The Ghost
and the Machine

Adam kept a vivid early memory of his outer layer peeled back and the circuitry and infrastructure underneath revealed to his still developing eye in what he took to be a lab: harsh lights, antiseptic stainless steel benches, tools and wires and bolts strewn about.

At the time he didn't know he was looking at himself, and he wondered how and why he happened to be viewing a mass of wiring and computer chips nestled in a cage supported by a honeycomb framework of bone-like material hidden in dark recesses.

Later he learned that a mirror on the wall happened to catch his reflection as the lab workers were powering up his sight circuitry. His vision held the image for a few moments, then it began to slide and blur. He fought to get it back, wanting to hold the picture as though it might reveal some crucial secret to him.

He heard beeps and feet shuffling. Some motion of white lab coats flashed across his field of view.

Then, a voice, much too loud: "Turn off the sense matrix. He's not ready yet."

Then nothing until his official resurrection when some white-coated woman, evidently a lab technician, welcomed him back to the world.

"Your systems all appear to be operating correctly," she said. "Our scans indicate that you have fastened yourself to the interior anchors. Can you confirm this for us?"

By some miracle Adam knew exactly what the technician was referring to. His phantom presence had, indeed, found purchase on some sort of structure. He had the sensation of being high up somewhere, looking down, which was disconcerting for a moment, then seemed perfectly right.

He felt like a trapeze performer hugging the pole after traversing the wire. It was not an unpleasant sensation. He found he felt at home in the strangest place he could ever have imagined.

He even had a voice. "Yes," he said, surprised by his own word.

"Good," said the technician, now peering at him from a short distance away. "My name's Amy. I'm your welcoming committee. You're our first complete success. How does it feel?"

How did it feel? To be dead one instant, then back in the world the next?

It felt strangely normal. Like he had been in this position before. Like he would be in this position forever if need be.

"What am I doing here?" he asked. "I remember dying. That car swerved into me. Head on. Some jerk on his cell phone, I think."

"Actually," said Amy, "I saw the report. No cell phone. He was drunk."

"Oh," said Adam. "Did he die, too?"

"Yes, I believe so."

"Did you bring *him* back?"

"No."

"Good. Some people should stay dead."

A pause. Long silence. "You seem to have strong feelings about it," said Amy. That last sentence almost a question, like she was gathering data.

"Not really," said Adam. "Just seems like the proper attitude to such things. Don't you agree?"

"I'm much more interested in your opinions," she said.

"Did you create me?"

"No. I'm just the gal in the lab."

"My Eve?"

"Hardly. Not God, either, if that's what you're thinking."

Adam did not have that in mind, but found himself wondering why she thought he might. There was more to this than he thought.

"I was really dead?"

"Yes. For several years. Do you remember any of it—the in between part, I mean?"

He didn't. Not a scarp. "No," he said flatly.

"We thought that might be the case," said Amy. "A lot of people are going to disappointed, though. They wanted to know what heaven was like."

"I can't help them."

"You're not obligated to," said Amy.

"Good. Are you going to hold me here forever?"

"No. You'll have an orientation period. Some robotic physical therapy to acclimate yourself to your prosthetic."

"Prosthetic?"

"A complete prosthetic. All your limbs are artificial. Your whole body is artificial. We've fitted this device to your essential being."

"Call me Frankenstein's monster, huh?"

Amy frowned at him. "We can't keep you from doing that, if it's really what you want, but it might not be to your benefit. You had a name. Adam. No reason you can't stick with that."

Yes, of course. Why not keep the name he grew up with? Still, a new name for a new existence was not out of the question. Except he still felt like an Adam. He looked at her, and for the first time noticed her face: kind and caring. Probably a good thing. Wouldn't want someone cold and dismissive welcoming back people from the other side.

He decided she was right. He would stay Adam. "How long have you guys been doing this sort of thing?" he asked.

"Not long." A pause. "You're the first complete success."

"Well, it looks like you know what you're doing. I already feel at home."

"That's terrific," said Amy. "In a while there'll be a whole team of people here to examine you and test you and all that. It'll be pretty exhausting. They thought you should see someone one-on-one to begin with. Less traumatic."

"A pretty face to welcome me to the world?"

Amy blushed. "Something like that," she said.

"I'm a ghost, aren't I?"

"In a manner of speaking."

Adam explored his interior. There were nooks and crannies everywhere. His—whatever it was: ghost, spirit, phantom, spook, smoke, apparition, *something*—crawled around in there and sent out tendrils of awareness all over the place, like fog invading a cave and hanging up on protuberances.

Those bumps of circuitry and mechanical bits were leverage points from where he was able to exert pressure that then swiveled his head, moved his limbs, and focused and unfocused his eyes, among other things. He exerted his will *here* and his arm swung up. Pressed his ghostly presence *there* and his head tilted to the side. Oomphed a tendril of his being onto another point and his vision blurred and then refocused. He lifted his hand and looked at it.

"I'm a ghost in a machine."

"Don't jump to any conclusions about yourself, yet," said Amy. "Let yourself get used to your new life first, then put labels on the whole thing."

"You probably shouldn't have done this," he said.

"Why do you say that?"

"Bringing people back from the dead. It's kind of crazy. Maybe—I don't know—wrong. Sinful. I'm looking for a word."

"Sacrilegious?"

"Yes, that's it."

"We've been accused of that."

"And what do you think of that accusation?"

"I let it roll off my back. Your parents wanted this."

"Really?"

"Yes."

"Where are they?"

"All in good time," said Amy. "We want them to be ready and you to be ready."

"How you going to make them ready for this? It's like I'm a clanking monster come to some kind of awful animated life."

"Actually, we have worked to reduce the noise of your

workings. Your limbs and accessories will operate almost noiselessly."

That information gave Adam very little comfort. Over the next few days he worked with Amy and half a dozen other technicians to come to fully understand the workings of his robot being.

He learned to walk, bend, lift things, and generally operate his robotic outer self in a competent manner. All the while he waited to see his parents.

Then, about a week into his therapy, word came from them. They had decided they could not see him in his present condition.

They were sorry, but their emotional selves could not face him as a robot.

Members of Adam's team scrambled to assist him in assimilating this information and keeping it from harming him emotionally.

Adam took the information in stride. After all, he understood it completely. Hadn't he told Amy, almost from the first, that he was unnatural? Hadn't be been bright enough to see the truth before anyone else?

Adam enrolled in a small college in Eastern Washington State, a land of dry yellow fields and big open skies, with numerous ranches and farms populating the countryside. His campus, a rambling collection of low-built structures set in a bucolic expanse of neatly-trimmed grass and an abundance of oak, cedar, and fruit trees, some wild, but many planted years ago, appealed to his newly found need for serenity. It seemed the perfect setting from where he could rally his faculties and come to some accommodation with his freshly reborn state of being.

He quickly settled on architecture as his major and reveled in the classes and course work until they assigned him to read the Bible.

This distressed Adam. Not because he had anything against the Bible. Not at all. He understood that it contained the source of much of Western culture and that, as an aspiring architect, he needed to understand this influence before he should be allowed to add to the culture with designed objects as visible and long-lived as buildings. His objection was the length of the book.

How could he find time to read its many dense pages between classes, homework, projects, assignments, and trivial matters like power consumption and maintenance dormancy?

His classmates devised schemes to get through the Bible. They formed study groups in which each member of the group had to read 200 pages of the Bible, then write a concise one or two page summary of those pages for the rest of the group to read and thereby absorb the information, plot, characters, and wisdom of the Bible.

By the time Adam was aware of such groups, they had

already assigned their pages and had no room for him. They most likely would not have made room for him anyway. Most of his fellow students shunned Adam, thinking of him as a particularly creepy presence. Not that Adam noticed this at first. Or even after a while.

This was a constant problem for Adam during his college years. He never knew what was going on until it was too late, an entirely understandable consequence of his circumstances, involving, as they did, his resurrection from his previous state into his present state, which most people did not fully understand.

He was sometimes called a mechanical zombie, which was not entirely inaccurate, but at the same time, seriously inadequate. It would have been more accurate to call him a hybrid zombie, since much of his interior was circuitry, not mechanics, except for his joints and limbs, of course. But even that was not quite right since he was no zombie. He had no flesh, dead or alive. He was pure spirit piloting a robot.

Adam's classmates called him a loner and a future absent-minded professor. This was enough to dismiss him from their minds. Adam was not precisely bothered by this, but it did prevent him from developing strong relationships with most people.

Adam believed in doing his assignments. He read the Bible. Every page, every word. Even all the begats.

He stayed up through the night for weeks in a row to finish it. Some of it, despite his having been part of the culture previously, were so foreign that he found he had to read pages several times to absorb their meaning.

His other courses suffered. His sanity took a hit for the worse. After all, the Bible is stuffed full of horrific events: plagues, murder, incest, death, smiting from above, gallons of blood spilling onto the desert sand. It was not enough that no such blood coursed through Adam's being: he still found the whole narrative decidedly distasteful and more than a little distressing.

None of that mattered. He was assigned to read the Bible, and by God!, he was going to read the Bible.

By the time he reached the end, Adam was thoroughly disgusted with humanity and deity alike. It may be that his preference to be somewhat removed from the everyday hustle and bustle of human life may have dated from this time. He requested an appointment with his teacher, Professor Barometer, to discuss his reaction to the Bible.

Barometer offered him fifteen minutes on a Friday afternoon. Adam accepted, and arrived at his appointment early and waited outside the professor's office door. He heard voices coming from inside the office. And laughter.

This indicated to Adam that another student was there, maybe trying to impress the professor. He wanted this other student to go. Adam had much more important matters to attend to with the professor.

A few minutes later the other student exited the office and walked down the hall, not even acknowledging Adam.

Such was the tenor of his relationship with all the other students. They knew he was different. It was not just his decidedly odd appearance or his awkward gait when he walked. It was the way he asked odd questions that none of them ever even considered. For example, during one lecture, he wanted to know from which mine the steel that went into the making of the Empire State Building was excavated. The professor didn't know.

Adam's opinion of that professor dropped a couple of notches. Another time, Adam wondered aloud, so that the rest of the class could hear, about which company it was that manufactured the paint that is used on the Golden Gate Bridge. Were they the original manufacturers? Did that company that now produced the paint allow students to come to the manufacturing facility and observe the process of making the paint? Again, the rest of the class shifted uncomfortably in their seats upon hearing Adam's voice.

Adam decided, at that time, that any friends he might find among his classmates would be rare indeed. He therefore felt no loss that Friday afternoon as the other student walked away from the professor's office without so much as a nod in Adam's direction.

Adam waited politely for about a minute, then knocked on the door.

"Come in." Barometer's voice.

Adam pushed the door open and stepped inside and carefully closed it behind him. Professor Barometer rose from behind her desk. "Adam, is it?"

"Yes, Professor." Adam noted a slight discomfort in the professor, but was also pleased to see that she made efforts to hide that discomfort.

"You're part of the resurrection program, aren't you?" she asked.

Well, yes, he was. What a strange question. Wasn't that obvious? Didn't she see that he was different from everyone else? Most decidedly different. Also, all faculty were fully apprised of Adam's presence on campus. Surely the professor knew this.

Adam worked through the ramifications of the question, then realized the professor was simply making conversation, something he himself used to do on occasion. Before he became a ghost. He remembered that he once enjoyed pushing air over his larynx and charging the atmosphere with his soundings. It was a characteristically human thing to want to do and the professor was obviously human. Now, of course, his voice, or the robot's voice which Adam animated, sounded very little like a human voice.

The techs had tried to make it natural, but the taint of electronic sound had not been thoroughly scrubbed from it. Adam had accepted this little fact. Not everyone he met was so accommodating, and it often led to encounters in which people deliberately tried to ignore the difference, fooling no one. Once Adam put all this into perspective, he was able to see his professor's remarks as a social nicety.

"Smoke and mirrors," said Adam. "That's me."

The professor raised her eyebrows.

"It's what I call myself," said Adam. "My spirit, the ghost inside me, what they called back from the dead, that's the smoke."

"And the mirrors?"

Adam straightened himself to emphasize his shiny exterior. "Well, just take a look. Can't you see yourself in my chest?"

The professor leaned slightly forward and peered into Adam's cool white skin, a construct of metal, plastic, and carbon, buffed to a gleaming sheen.

"Now that you mention it," said the professor.

Adam shrugged. "It's a look they wanted to cultivate—the people who started this whole thing. They thought the public would like it. Shiny and clean, you know. Not disgusting at all."

"They really thought of that?"

"They thought of a lot of things I wouldn't have thought of. I'm thinking of having the shine removed, though. It's disconcerting sometimes to see people looking at themselves while looking at you."

"I can imagine. They did a remarkable job with your face, though."

"They spent a lot of time on that. Fake skin that looks

pretty real, I'm told. They tried to get all the expressions in with little motors manipulating the spongy fake flesh underneath the skin."

"They seem to care about you. How you are presented and perceived."

"I suppose so," said Adam. "They think of themselves as creators. Kind of like Gods."

"Not an altogether incorrect view, given what they did."

"Well, see, I think that's where you might be wrong. They didn't create anything, not like God did, who started with nothing, basically, and created everything. The ones who put me together, they *copied*. Copied existing anatomy, copied natural modes of communication, copied ways of locomotion. Very clever, what they did, I'm not discounting that, but not gods. Or if you wanted to really press the point, I might concede that they are mediocre gods. At best."

"I take your point. We are all less than divine, aren't we?"

"Exactly."

"Are you glad you volunteered for the program?"

How could people be so ignorant? Didn't this professor follow the news at all? Dead people did not "volunteer" to be resurrected. "Actually," said Adam, "they never asked if I wanted to be part of the program. I was assigned to it, in a way. That is, my family decided to participate." How much detail should he give in explaining his circumstance? Adam did not know what was appropriate, but decided to forgo caution and plunge in.

"What actually happened was that my parents were somewhat devastated by my death, so they grasped at any straw that might give them comfort. They went to seances. They investigated life after death gurus. And ended up approaching these researchers that were using ghost energy to animate robots. And so, here I am. A ghost in a machine. They never asked me. Well, how could they? I was dead, and the technology was new. Primitive. They just assumed I'd *want* to come back. Because I was so young when I died. Too young. See, I was driving the interstate, and some guy crossed over the median in the opposite direction and I couldn't swerve out of his way and—Boom!—I was gone. It's more tragic when someone young dies, isn't it? After you put on a few years, the tragic aspect of it diminishes quite a bit. People aren't quite so sad after you get to a certain age." As soon as the rush of words left his anatomical construct, Adam noted that it might be too much information for the social interaction at hand. After all, idle conversation was not meant to bring up deep secrets. It was meant to make people comfortable with each other.

"Do you regret what they did?"

"I resent not being asked."

"But as you said, they couldn't ask. It sounds like they did it for love."

Love? Maybe. They needed to assuage their pain. Adam understood that. But now that he was back, they didn't really love him. Who could love a hunk of hardware, even one animated by spirit? "Love is a complex thing," he said. "Many ramifications in that one little word. They could possibly love me in the way someone loves their car. But not in the way a parent loves a child."

The professor looked momentarily mystified, then regained her composure quickly. "Yes, of course," she said.

"It's complicated," said Adam.

Barometer nodded. "Life itself is full of complexities, isn't it? No matter how we got here."

Adam nodded.

"I must say," said the professor, "you are an interesting presence in my classroom."

"Thank you," said Adam instantly. He was fully aware that the comment might not have been complimentary, but he decided to manipulate the conversation to some extent in an attempt to make himself appear more favorable. He understood this to be a method of attracting good things to himself.

"Someone in your position. Well, I was just wondering, your life, your—resurrection—has made you an historical figure. One of the most significant people in the history of the world, and yet you choose to pursue an architectural degree." She spread her hands as if to say: "What's up with that, guy? Are you a crazy man?"

"But professor," he said, "you yourself *teach* architecture. Do you not consider it worthy?"

"It simply seems that pursuing any degree, for you, must be kind of—prosaic. Mundane."

"After you get over the initial 'wow!' factor of how I came back, my life is pretty dull. I had aspirations for architecture before I died. I was always building things as a kid. When I came back, my advisors said it might be most beneficial if I tried to get back to a normal life. Pursuing my studies again seemed as normal as it gets."

She nodded. "Are you finding your time here fruitful?" She was studying him. He saw that. She was fascinated by him. As who wouldn't be? He was unique on campus, probably unique in the world.

"It is difficult at times," said Adam.

"I'm sorry you are not liking it."

"I don't necessarily dislike it. I was merely letting you know that things are not always what one might expect, and then a bit of disappointment sets in which requires a readjustment of one's expectations. I was fully apprised of such eventualities when I got fused with my robot."

"Aah," said the professor.

"One must accept what is."

The professor nodded. "Wise words indeed."

Adam had been in other professor's offices. Most of them had piles of papers everywhere and shelves lined with books. Barometer had none of these. Her desk was immaculate: not a scrap of paper, only a small notebook computer in one corner. Her walls were adorned with large framed photos of buildings. Not skyscrapers, which is what Adam would have expected, but instead a series of small buildings. Tiny houses. A minuscule public library. An outhouse. A medium-sized barn.

"What can I do for you today?" She said. "Do you need some help with the work? I see you slipped a little on your last mid-term."

"Uh, yes," said Adam. "I wanted to mention that. You see, I had to let the rest of my work slide a little because I had to read the Bible and then you never mentioned it in class and I wanted to know why you made me spend all that time with it if you weren't even going to bring it up. Seems like a waste, so I wanted to hear your take on it."

Professor Barometer looked surprised. "You read the whole thing?"

Adam nodded.

"You certainly *are* different, then. I don't think any of my students have ever read the whole Bible. Not that I ever heard of, anyway."

Adam felt instantly foolish. His smoke froze in place, and with it, his exoskeleton. He watched Professor Barometer's expression change from attentive interest to slight amusement at his expense.

"But I thought," said Adam. "That is, you *assigned* the Bible. It was on the reading list."

"Well, there's lots of items on the reading list. We don't expect you to read every word. I would think a few hours spent skimming it, getting a feel for the flavor of the work, would be sufficient."

"There was nothing to indicate that approach to the material."

"We don't tell you everything. We expect you to have the ability to see what you need to do thoroughly, and what you can do with a little less—shall we say—diligence. For example, there are concise study aids to the Bible. I know many students just skim that, which seems to work out fine. It's all about balance. However, it appears that I might be more explicit in the future. For the benefit of those such as yourself." She smiled again.

Adam's mind reeled under this new information. There was a much less modest expectation of him than he had thought. How could this be? Didn't he need to understand the material thoroughly? He was going to be designing important buildings. Didn't he need the most rigorous training possible?

"I will attempt to understand the concept of balance in the future," he said.

"I think it'll do you good. I'll make a confession to you. I haven't read every word of every book on the list. Part of what you are supposed to learn here is how to absorb information quickly and efficiently. That isn't always by reading every word of a document. Do you understand?"

"So you're saying that I don't need to do what you ask me to do? Can I just skim the final exam, get a feel for the flavor of the questions, and let it go at that? Would such an approach get me an A in your course Professor?"

Professor Barometer put her hands together and brought her finger tips to her chin. "Are you upset with me? Because there's no reason to be. I'm not saying you *can't* read the whole thing. Be my guest if that's what you want to do. I'm just saying there may be other ways to manage the work load."

Adam wanted to speak up. He wanted to tell Professor Barometer that it would have been nice if she had mentioned this skimming business and this information absorbing theory earlier in the semester. Perhaps even in the syllabus. But he knew if he talked now he would begin to stammer from the embarrassment and the acute stress he was feeling simply by being in the Professor's office and being made to feel so ridiculous.

His smoke's connection to his hardware sometimes slipped its moorings a little when he felt this way. Instead, his entire demeanor deflated. He settled slightly deeper into his chair and his shoulders slumped and his head swiveled slightly down on its neck stalk.

"Tell you what," said Professor Barometer. "Since you did read the whole thing, every word, as you said, I'll give you five points on your final grade over and above what you earn from your assignments and exams. How does that suit you?"

It suited Adam fine. He nodded.

Professor Barometer spread her hands. "All right then. Will there be anything else?"

"I," said Adam, then stopped.

"Yes," said Professor Barometer.

"I. I-I-I." Adam closed his eyes, trying to find some purchase on the world, trying to get his words to engage with reality, but they skittered over the surface like birds trying to land on sheets of ice, fluttering and squeaking incoherently.

He opened his eyes, expecting to see concern on the professor's face, but she presented only a calm and expectant attitude. It was as though she was waiting for a child to finish eating its pablum. He worked to link his smoke to his mirror, a slippery business that sometimes required his full attention.

"Take your time," she said. "I know this sort of thing is difficult for some students."

There was no audible click, but a familiar connection reasserted itself, gave him a jolt of energy, and he spoke up. "I now hate God," he said, blurting out the words like they were poison he had to get out of his system.

The professor, evidently startled by this assertion, remained silent for several seconds while Adam worked to formulate more words to fill the emptiness, but could find nothing inside him. It was as though his confession cleared everything else away.

"I see," said the professor, finally. "When did that happen?"

"As I was reading the Bible. I never hated God before.

Then you gave us this assignment, and it changed everything."

"Well, I'm sure you must have a more complex relationship with God than the rest of us. After all, you've seen the other side, as it were. And come back."

"There's nothing there," said Adam. "Let me assure you of that."

"Nothing?"

"A blankness unlike anything you could ever imagine."

"I've read some accounts which say there is an afterlife, but that people—like you—who get called back, simply don't remember that afterlife. You claim blankness because your brains created the blankness."

"Those accounts were not written by anyone who has gone through the process. Totally idle speculation. Unworthy of attention."

"I see."

He did not want this to become another discussion about himself. He was tired of talking about himself. Yes, he was a miracle of modern day technology. But isn't everyone a miracle? Isn't the sprouting of fully formed beings from the coupling of an egg and a sperm cell, isn't *that* a miracle?

Every pregnant woman who ever lived understood that. Adam was not even close to that. He was a trick of electronics and ether. Nothing more. "Professor," he said, "I don't want to hate God. It does me no good and it fills me with despair."

"You're saying you used to love God. Is that it?"

Adam considered the question. Why did she bring up love again? Love was a strong word. He wasn't sure he would go that far, but he did know that he had not been interested in doing away with God, not before. But now, that was exactly how he felt about the situation.

"I never even thought about God much before this."

"Really? Don't young people usually think about God at some point? I know I did when I was about sixteen. It consumed my thoughts for weeks. Is there a God? Isn't there? How can one know for sure?" She smiled.

"I never did that. I never thought about God before. Ever."

"So you remember your past life?"

"Of course. I just don't remember the in between part."

"What kind of young man were you?"

"The normal kind. Nothing special. I was getting ready to apply for college."

"Which is why you decided to continue."

"Yes."

"Did you have a girlfriend?"

"I don't see how that's relevant."

"Just curious," said Barometer.

"Just curious," said Adam, attempting to mimic her voice, but failing miserably. He sounded shrill instead of defiant.

"I was just wondering what you did instead of thinking about the big questions that so many young people seem to take up with passion. Were you too busy having fun? Sports, maybe? Video games?"

"Not exactly. I had a girlfriend, but she's not important anymore. We could never be together again. Not with me like this. I had a family, too. They're not important either. I even had a dog. Also no longer important. As for religion, it just never came up. We weren't a religious family so I never thought about religious matters."

"Okay. And now?"

"I think about God all the time. I think about how people say he is a supreme being, and how he is the embodiment of love. And so on. But, Professor, it is awful what God does."

"I've heard him called 'the supreme fascist.'"

Adam clicked his fingers and straightened his hardware. "Yes, yes, Professor. That's exactly it. He has a most peculiar notion of love, this God, the way he contrives to bring down calamities on those he professes to care about." Adam paused. He needed time to formulate his next thought. The professor seemed to understand this. She waited patiently for him, neither encouraging nor hindering his progress. Adam recognized her approach as the Socratic Method, in which the teacher, rather than actively imparting information, contrives to allow the student to dredge it up from the ether himself. "What I mean to say, Professor, is that I blame you entirely for my current depressive state and for my need to release the knowledge that you have, through your assignment, thrust upon me."

"I will accept some responsibility for opening your eyes to possibilities you had not considered previously," said the Professor. "But you accepted the assignments when you enrolled in my course. You chose to pursue the assignment in your own way. And you—*only* you—decided to take the information from this ancient collection of tales, and use it to make yourself miserable."

Well. That was direct and unequivocal. Adam did not expect such an answer from Professor Barometer. He felt deflated and ridiculous. Again.

She was like God, wasn't she? Making him feel less than he could be. Making him feel like he had no real power over himself.

Yes, he chose to do certain things, but in the end, those things had their own power. He could not overcome what they did to him.

"I suppose," he said, "I must accept what you are telling me, but shouldn't knowing this give me a feeling of power?"

The professor smiled at him. "Power comes from many places," she said. "But the only real power is what comes from yourself. I suggest you try to ignore many of these big questions about God and what he means. Bigger minds than ours have struggled with these issues and have not come up with any conclusions. The reading assignment was meant to open your eyes to some of the influences on our culture. Nothing more. They run pretty deep, you know. It is to your advantage to be aware of them."

Adam pondered her words for a few moments, then realized he was being dismissed. It was subtle, to be sure, but these, surely, were words she was hoping would be the last between them for now.

Adam abruptly stood. "Thank you for your time Professor Barometer."

She nodded. "Of course."

He stood.

"One thing, if you don't mind," said Professor Barometer.

"Yes?"

"May I have my picture taken with you? My daughter would appreciate it. She thinks a ghost who comes back from the dead to live in a robot is—well, to put it in her words—'the awesomest.'"

Adam searched through his instructions for how to answer this request. Should he acquiesce? Should he refuse?

His counselors did not offer much guidance on this issue. They wanted the returnees to make some decisions on their own.

Which, come to think of it, is how he got into trouble with this Bible business.

"Some people think we're evil," said Adam.

"Ignorant people. You can't be evil unless you do evil acts. Have you done anything evil since your return?"

"No, Professor."

"How about before your return?"

"You mean when I was alive?"

"Yes."

Adam thought back. How could he? He was too young to do anything truly evil.

He had lived a normal middle class life, with the requisite adolescent rebellion, but definitely nothing truly *bad*.

"No, Professor," he said. "Certainly nothing like some of the things God did in that book you made me read."

He tried to keep his face from betraying any emotion, but was aware some of the robot's automatic mechanisms discerned an attempt at humor in his words and contrived to contort his face—ever so slightly—into a subtle grin, as though letting the professor know he was self aware of his own humor.

"How about between?"

"You mean while I was dead?"

She nodded, then stopped herself. "I forgot, you don't remember."

"That's right."

"But you were dead. How could you have done anything that could be called evil, right?"

"Right," said Adam.

"You had no way of interacting with this world."

Not quite correct. The ghosts did have a very slight influence, though it was so minuscule it took one of the brightest minds of the day to discover and exploit it.

"None that mattered," said Adam.

"Well, then," she said brightly, "we're all good. Let me get my camera."

Adam's advisor, the man assigned to help Adam adapt to his new circumstances, was named Charlie. Perfect. And everyman name for someone to turn Adam in an everyday man. Adam liked Charlie well enough, although he thought sometimes he was more interested in the project than he was in Adam as an independent being. Adam supposed that was to be expected. The project was, after all, bigger than just himself.

Adam arrived at his scheduled appointment session a little late, on purpose. Just to remind Charlie that he had some autonomy of his own and meant to exercise it whenever he could. The meeting took place in a park near Charlie's office. The people who ran the project thought this would be better than a sterile building environment.

Charlie sat on a bench near a pond. His briefcase leaned against the bench and he had a paper bag in his hand from which he grabbed handfuls of corn kernels and tossed them to the ground for a flock of pigeons that clustered around him. As Adam approached the bench, the pigeons, cooing and fluttering, flowed away from him and did not return, even though Charlie rustled the kernels in the bag with his hand.

"I haven't seen you in a while," said Charlie.

"I've been a busy student."

"Yes, and how is that going?"

"I had a most peculiar meeting with my architecture professor."

"Oh. Please tell me about it." He pulled a brown bag out of his briefcase, and retrieved a wrapped sandwich from it. He began pulling the waxed paper off the sandwich as he leaned in expectantly toward Adam. Adam's ears felt like they were under assault from all the rustling, snapping, and popping of the waxed paper.

"First off," he said, "I need you to adjust my hearing."

"Your hearing?"

"Everything is too loud."

"I see. Hang on." He put down his sandwich and got a cell phone from the briefcase and fired up the app that controlled Adam's parameters. He fiddled with the thing for a few seconds while Adam waited patiently. "I've got you set for acute hearing," he said. "How about we drop it down to intermediate?"

"Please."

Charlie's finger tip danced across the screen rapidly. "How's that?"

Adam turned his head to take in the park sounds: wind rustling over trees, more birds calling, voice of people in the park as they walked by. He still heard them all, but not as loudly as before.

"Much better," he said.

"Good. You know you can call me anytime and I'll take care of little things like this."

"I don't want to bother you," said Adam.

"It's no bother. This is my job. I'm here to make your life work for you as best we can."

"It's crazy that I can't control my own hearing."

"Yes. A kind of odd glitch they never quite fixed. They're supposed to get it taken care of in the next generation of robots. But, like I said, I'll take care of things like this. Happily."

"You're saying you care about me."

"Why yes, Adam, I do."

Adam wasn't sure this was true. This was a job for Charlie and if he wasn't drawing a paycheck Adam was pretty sure he would have no interest in maintaining a relationship with Adam. But he did not challenge Charlie on the subject, seeing no upside to it. Instead he pursued another point. "Do you think what they did to me—well, do you think it was evil?"

Charlie put up his hands. "Whoa," he said. "Where did that come from? They gave you a new life."

"On their terms."

"Well, what terms should they have employed? What other way is there?"

"They could have asked me."

"But they couldn't. You know that. It's not just you. No one has ever been asked if they want to be born."

"I wasn't born. I was reborn."

"It amounts to the same thing, in a way."

Of course, of course. Adam knew that. "It still feels wrong," said Adam.

"They asked your family," said Charlie.

"Oh, yeah. My family. You know neither of my parents spends any time with me at all. When I asked if I could come over for a visit, they made excuses. To their son, excuses. I've stopped asking."

Charlie listened attentively, though he reserved some of his attention for his sandwich, chewing with gusto, which Adam found a little disgusting. All that squishy mashing and slurping.

"I'm afraid they have pulled away from the project quite a bit," said Charlie. "It was not what they expected. You were not what they expected."

"Do you ever talk to Dr. Deed?" Deed was the chief scientist involved with discovering unequivocal evidence of ghosts while running an experiment on a super collider. He found the ghost of some unknown rabbit, which died during the construction of the super collider, and which he named Ether, curled around one of the trails left by the collisions of numerous sub-atomic particles. It was decidedly not what he had expected to find, there in the intricate trails left by those particles. The discovery catapulted him to fame and prompted him to refine his discovery until he was able to find and manifest the ghosts of people. All that remained after that was to find a way to allow the ghosts to communicate.

He teamed up with a Dr. Finale, an expert on artificial intelligence, who had developed a robot which could animate itself, but which lacked a true mind. Enter Dr. Deed and his ghosts. The two mad scientist worked in secret for a year, devising the interface systems that would eventually connect Deed's ghosts with Finale's robots. The chief difficulty was amplifying the incredibly tiny amount of energy that made up a ghost.

Eventually they succeeded and immediately began to offer their service to the public. Bring back your dead, was their slogan, which was not the best choice. They got takers, Adam's parents among them, but far fewer than they had hoped for. And there were difficulties.

The resurrection was not always successful. The older the subject, the less chance of success. Also, if the ghost had a difficult health history during its life, resurrection was impossible. Something about illness damaged the spirit. Someone like Adam, who died of a trauma quickly and young, was the best candidate possible.

"I've met him only once," said Charlie. "He's very reclusive. A very odd kind of man, if I may say so. He said he liked me because I was real."

"I guess then he doesn't like me," said Adam.

"Why?"

"I'm not real. Look at me."

"Now, Adam. We talked about this. You're different, but that doesn't mean you aren't every bit as important as any person. Any *being* for that matter."

"They really messed with nature, you know."

Charlie finished his sandwich and wiped his mouth with a paper napkin and mashed it up in the waxed paper until he had a compact round ball. Adam saw this as stalling for time. It made him think of Professor Barometer. She stalled for time, too, while taking the measure of him. Lots of people, when they were around Adam, treated him like he was an anomaly. Maybe like some horribly disfigured or disabled person that they had to carefully tiptoe around, lest they offend him inadvertently.

"A lot of what people do is not exactly natural," said Charlie. "I don't need to tell you that. You're studying architecture, for God's sake. About the most unnatural pursuit there is, manipulating nature to create shelter for human beings. Civilization itself is not natural. You are merely the latest step in a million year continuum of humans bending nature to their will. It started with fire, probably, in some cave somewhere, and it's been going strong ever since."

"Is that supposed to comfort me?"

Charlie laughed. It was a genuine laugh, Adam had to give him that. It was not faked or strained. "Something like that," he said.

"He's like my father, you know."

"Deed?"

"Yes. It's like both my father's want nothing to do with me."

"Well, I wouldn't take it personally, Adam. He keeps to himself, like I told you. It's nothing against you. He's just very socially awkward."

"So he creates socially awkward constructs to make himself feel better?"

"No, no. He and Finale, they just want to help people now."

"I don't think so. I think maybe they both should have stuck to sub atomic particles and not messed around with people." Adam stood up. Charlie looked startled.

"Are you leaving?"

"You haven't even asked me about school."

"I did, Adam. When you first came."

"If I had been asked, and if I had known what was going to happen, I never would have agreed to come back. And dammit, I can't even cry. They going to put that capacity in the new models?"

Adam turned quickly, too quickly, and got his feet caught in the grass and began to keel over. Fortunately, motion detectors in his torso, head, and joints immediately activated and quickly shifted his weight and balance in the proper direction to keep him from falling. But Adam *wanted* to fall. Falling was part of life, part of being human, and here this gizmo he was trapped inside wouldn't allow him the simple courtesy of allowing him to commit a simple common mistake.

Charlie stood up and put his hands on Adam's gleaming exterior, hoping to help him stay upright. Adam felt the pressure of Charlie's palms and understood what they signified, that Charlie did indeed see him as worthy of consideration. But it was a kind of consideration Adam had grown to resent.

"Are you okay?" said Charlie.

"I'm sick of school," said Adam. "All I want to do now is find Bibles wherever I can, put them all into a giant pile, and burn them."

Despite his proclamation, Adam finished architecture school, though his experience of reading the Bible haunted all his days on campus. He received his degree on a particularly warm July afternoon in an outdoor ceremony along with hundreds of other graduates.

The sun heated his skin on that day, which his sensors registered as a pleasing sensation, and his parents were not present. Neither were Drs. Deed or Finale. Adam expected that they were probably involved in some new scheme, like creating hamster zombies or some such. He didn't care. He curled his carbon fingers around his diploma as it was handed to him, then walked off the stage and into a mass of reporters holding microphones, and camera operators shining lights on him.

"That's going to put a nasty glare in your picture," he said to one of the camera operators, who then peeked out from behind the view finder.

"We've got a filter," she said.

"Good thinking," said Adam. He turned to the assembled members of the electronic press. "So, what are you all doing here?"

"Can you tell us your plans?" said a face behind a microphone.

"I'm considering my options," said Adam.

"Have you gotten job offers? We heard that Goodrich and Hastings is interested in you."

G and H did indeed extend an offer to Adam, even before his senior year, but Adam did not like what they did. They were mostly interested in designing skyscrapers, attempting to beat the world record for tall buildings.

He perceived that they weren't truly interested in him as an architectural talent, but in having him on their staff as an example of a technological marvel they could own and exploit. While he had not formally turned down their offer, neither had he told them to forget it. He found he liked having people interested in him, no matter what their motive.

"I haven't done anything, you know. All I did was get a diploma." He held it up for everyone to see.

The cameras tilted up. That would make a good image: a

mechanical hand holding a piece of paper: new technology married to old technology.

"You're immortal," said another reporter. "How does that feel?"

"Creepy," said Adam, still holding the diploma high. Charlie came up behind him and put a hand on his back. Adam felt the palm and felt Charlie nudge him to the side. Charlie didn't want Adam to be talking to these reporters. Charlie always advised him to stay away from publicity as much as possible. The idea was to lead as normal a life as possible. Fame was not a normal life. Adam usually paid attention to Charlie, but not this time.

Another reporter spoke up. "Dr. Deed, your resurrector, was not here for the ceremony," he said. "Are you disappointed."

"A little," said Adam.

"Why do you think he didn't come?"

"He's a wrinkled old man," said Adam. "He didn't want to witness my youthful accomplishment because he can't stand that he'll die and I won't."

"What about your parents?"

"What about them?"

"They didn't come either."

"You'll have to ask them about that," said Adam.

Charlie decided to assert his power, such as it was. "All right, folks," he said. "You got what you wanted. Let Adam celebrate with his classmates."

"We heard they don't like Adam."

"That's not true," said Charlie.

"No," said Adam. "It is true. I don't like them either. Ever since I came back, I've had this emptiness in my inner being."

Charlie groaned. Adam heard him. He didn't care.

"Can you elaborate on this emptiness?" said one of the reporters.

Adam paused. For dramatic effect. "Even God couldn't stand emptiness," said Adam. "Even he was struck with terror when he perceived the nothingness around him. The Bible doesn't mention that, the terror, but it was there. So God filled it up with creation. With the natural world you see all around us and with us. You and me."

"Are you equating yourself with God?"

"Why not?" said Adam. "Can you prove I'm not?"

That caused a ripple of electricity to go around the little group. Adam felt it: a surge of interest in him. In his words. A queasy feeling tried to assert itself in his being. Adam quelled it immediately.

"Is that why you studied architecture? You want to create things? Because God is the ultimate creator? Do you want to be like him?"

Adam applied pressure to the leverage points that produced laughter. "You may be taking my words too literally," he said.

"The people that resurrected you haven't been able to resurrect anyone else, isn't that true?"

"I've heard as much," said Adam.

"So you're one of a kind."

"So far."

"Is that why you think you're God? Because there's no one else like you?"

"I think that's going too far," said Adam.

"So you're saying you *aren't* God?"

"Let's get off the God talk," said Adam.

"Yes," said Charlie, "let's leave God out of this." Adam wished Charlie would disappear. Adam knew how to handle himself with these reporters.

One of the other reporters spoke up. "Do you know what kind of buildings you want to create?"

"I've thought about that a lot," said Adam. "About creation. You don't just plunge into it you know. You have to consider a lot of things. I may take my time with it. After all, I have a lot of it. Time. I could plan a building for a hundred years before I decide to start making it."

"Is that what you intend to do?"

"I don't know," said Adam. "I only just graduated. Give me a little bit of time."

"Have you found love, yet?" said another reporter. "Do you have a girlfriend?"

"Girlfriend?" said Adam. "His face contorted into a grimace. "Are you kidding me? Who would go out with—" he indicated his glossy exterior by swooping both his hands down his shiny white sides "—this?"

The other reporters looked at the one who asked the last question as if he was an idiot.

"Well," said the reporter, "it's not completely out of the question. Even paraplegics have girl and boy friends. Lots of disabled people have—you know—relationships."

Embarrassed silence fell on the group. Adam's servomotors purred and hummed as his head swung around to face the reporter. Adam tilted his chest slightly forward, flexed his fingers to form fists, and took two steps forward that shook the ground. "Do I *look* disabled to you?" he said.

Then, from behind the mass of microphone-holding, glossy-haired, and shiny-minded media specialists, an old man with a long white beard and a stooped posture pushed his way forward, knocking people aside as if they were nothing but bits of trash. He got to the front of the group and looked up at Adam. His beard matched Adam's exterior: mostly white, but now with some gray spots from years of use.

"I heard you've got a thing for the Bible," said the old man.

"Who are you?" said Charlie.

"The name's Ilija," said the man. "I have a proposition for you."

"If it has anything to do with you," said Adam, "you can forget it."

"Maybe I can, but you can't. You're named Adam. The book practically starts with you."

Adam laughed. "I'm not that Adam," he said.

"How do you know?"

Charlie's hand was still on Adam's back, and it hung there, like it couldn't move. Like Charlie couldn't make it move. Everyone else went dead silent, either from the strange presence of this odd man, or from what he said. Adam wasn't sure which.

"I used to be a young man before a car killed me. I was not the Adam that Eve went with." He smiled. Still no one else said anything.

"The scientists," said Ilija, "that dug you up and tossed you inside that thing, they don't know. They only guess. Only you know. You could be the first Adam. Or you could be Eve. Yes. Or you could be an elephant. Or a bug. You could be anything at all. Any creature. You ever thought of that?"

"I have," said Adam. "But you're wrong. I know who I am. I'm me."

Except he didn't know. Not for sure. He could be anyone they found and brought back. They told him he was a young man who died unexpectedly and he believed them and he took the facts into his being and made them his own, but they weren't his own. Maybe he had succumbed to suggestions they offered him. Ghosts didn't come with name tags. They were just *there*. Maybe he was the original Adam. Or maybe—like Ilija said—he was a bug they found that had been squashed under someone's foot. Maybe he was nothing. Nothing at all.

"It's not like that," said Charlie to Ilija. "There are safeguards, independent corroboration parameters. We know who Adam is."

"Do you?" said Ilija.

"Yes," said Charlie.

The cameras swiveled from Charlie to Ilija. Ilija turned to Adam. "You say you do."

Adam nodded.

"Can you prove it?" said Ilija.

What a question. Adam was a mundane miracle of modern science. He was a trick concocted by mad scientists with delusions of godhood.

"I—" said Adam. "I-I-I." He felt tendrils of spirit loosening from their moorings inside his construct. Why was this happening now? He was here. He was a being named Adam, and he had extension and weight and consequence and, and, and.

And nothing.

He was nothing. A mere blip in the continuum of the universe. He gathered his being around him, in a focused attempt to *keep himself here and now* in front of this strange man. This elf-like thing.

"I am Adam," he said, with a degree of solemnity he had not intended.

A general buzz of excitement rose from the reporters, now shocked back into speech.

"Which Adam?" they all asked him, nearly at once.

"The Adam this man wants," said Adam.

Ilija extended his hand, a wrinkled and splotchy one, and held it out for a long time. Adam heard his internal motors hum as his shoulder moved and his elbow angled forward and his hand opened its fingers, dropping his diploma to the grass. He stepped forward, mashing the paper into the green blades, and curled his fingers as delicately as he could around Ilija's hand.

Ilija stared into Adam's eyes. He ignored his reflection in Adam's chest. No one had ever done that before. People always admired their reflection in Adam's robot skin. They liked to see themselves in his body.

But not Ilija. He riveted his attention onto Adam's face. Adam swiveled his visual sensors up and down in their housing, mimicking people who sometimes swiveled their eyes up and down in their sockets to take in Adam in all his artificial glory. He wanted to take in Ilija in all *his* natural glory.

There was something eternal about Ilija. He had a hills and valleys face, craggy and lined like a weathered landscape. It made Adam think of wind on his face. Rain in his eyes. The sun burning the top of his head.

"So what's your story, old man?" said Adam. "Why are you here on my graduation day?"

"I've got a proposition for you," said Ilija.

Adam's head hummed as it did a quarter turn and he leaned closer to Ilija. "I'm all ears," he said.

Ilija, in his younger days, had been all over the world, putting copies of the Bible into the hands of people who had never heard of the Bible. At least, that was the story he told Adam later that day, after Adam had bid farewell to the reporters and their questions and accompanied Ilija on a walk across campus. Charlie wanted to tag along, but Adam invoked his right of privacy, which Deed and Finale had made sure was built into him as a way of mimicking human nature, and told Charlie to find something else to do for a while. Charlie agreed, though reluctantly. He gave Ilija a look of withering contempt as Adam and Ilija parted his company. Ilija, if he noticed, did not indicate either dismay or amusement, much to Adam's satisfaction.

Ilija finished a dramatic story about being chased by ferocious tigers in the wilds of Africa, where he had been on a mission to put Bibles into the hands of some natives there. "That's how I spent my youth," said Ilija.

"That's quite a tale," said Adam.

They stopped walking. Adam saw that they were under a tree on the edge of campus. The tree bore orange fruit, heavy and ripe, that pulled the branches down toward the ground. They swayed gently in complex sideways and up and down motions, undulating in the wind. Adam imagined the tips of the branches fitted with paint brushes, executing paintings in the air.

"I was doing work that was bigger than me," said Ilija.

"Was it worth it?" asked Adam.

"Hell, yes," said Ilija, grinning. "The best thing I ever did. So far."

"How old are you?" said Adam.

"I'm in my ninth decade," said Ilija.

Adam wondered what a man of Ilija's age could look forward to that might qualify as the best thing he ever did.

"You probably don't have all that much time left," said Adam.

"True," said Ilija. "I want you to follow in my footsteps."

"But I don't like the Bible," said Adam. "It's depressing. Why would I spread copies of it around to people?"

"You came back for a reason," said Ilija.

"I came back because my parents are inconsiderate dolts, and the scientists they found are inconsiderate egoists."

"No, no," said Ilija. "Don't say such things about your parents."

"It's true."

"Doesn't matter if you think it's true."

"It matters to me."

"Your parents gave you life."

"Do you know anything of my history?" said Adam.

"I know you got called back from heaven."

"It wasn't heaven," said Adam.

"It was. You don't remember, but it was. It had to be. There is no other explanation."

"It must be nice to be so sure of everything."

"I'm sure you don't want to design buildings," said Ilija. "That's as clear as the man-made skin on your face."

"What do you know about my wants?" said Adam.

"Buildings are trivial. What you should be doing is building spirit. You would be an inspiration to many people. I'd start you out small. You could place Bibles in motel rooms. It's an easy thing to do. You find the manager and ask them if they have Bibles in their rooms. Most do, but some don't. So then you get to put one in each room. It's wonderful. It's an inspirational thing for many people to find Bibles in their motel rooms. Especially the way people end up in motel rooms. For illicit liaisons, sometimes. Or because their lives are a mess. They need the inspiration of the Bible."

Adam saw the man's point, but didn't see that the Bible was the way to achieve inspiration. "What about people who are just in the motel room because they need a place to stay for the night. They aren't liasoning illicitly or feeling depressed or anything."

"The Bible has wisdom for all," said Ilija.

"Have you read the Bible?" said Adam.

"Of course. Many times. I read parts of it daily."

"Why do you like it so much?"

"Adam, it's not a matter of liking. It's more a case of nourishment. It's the spiritual nutrition I need to keep going. I think it's the spiritual nutrition you need as well."

"Do you have one with you?"

Ilija grinned. "You bet I do."

"May I see it?"

Ilija, still grinning, reached into his back pocket and retrieved a slim paperback volume with ultra-thin pages. He held it up for Adam to see, obviously proud of it in the same way a parent displays pride when showing off their children's refrigerator art to visitors.

"You love your Bible," said Adam.

"I've had it for years," said Ilija. "It's the only thing I own that I would never ever part with."

Adam moved his hand closer to the Bible resting on Ilija's palm. "May I?" said Adam.

Ilija nodded.

Adam, with utmost delicacy, applied the tips of two of his fingers to either side of the volume and lifted it off Ilija's hand. He noted that Ilija had tears in his eyes, probably from the thought that he was imparting the wisdom of the ages to a machine.

Adam brought his other hand to the volume, as if preparing to open the cover and begin reading. Instead, with unwavering finality, he folded back the worn front cover, lifted up the first dozen pages or so, tore them smartly out of the binding, and began tearing the pages of Ilija's most prized possession into little confetti bits.

Ilija turned red immediately. The grin dropped from his face and he moved to grab the Bible back. But Adam simply raised his hands out of Ilija's reach and continued methodically tearing out pages and ripping them to shreds. The pieces of the bible, pure white pages with black and red lettering, fluttered up into the air and dispersed around them like snowflakes. Some of the pieces fell to the ground, others just kept rising on the wind. After a few moments, Ilija stopped trying to halt the exercise and simply watched the snowfall around him. Adam left no page whole. He converted every single one into tiny scraps, and when he was done, tore up the front and back cover for good measure.

Ilija's face registered despair, sorrow, grief, and pain. But no anger. At least not that Adam could discern.

"How about that?" said Adam. "Your precious Bible is nothing but litter now."

Tear tracks streaked Ilija's face. Adam noted this, but was not disturbed or disgusted. He actually liked this silly little man with his ridiculous ideas about the importance of his ridiculous book.

"Thank you," said Ilija in a harsh whisper.

Adam experienced consternation. He could not have heard that correctly. Maybe he needed to ask Charlie to raise his aural acuity again. "Did you say 'thank you?'" said Adam.

Ilija nodded.

"I just destroyed your most valued object in the world."

Ilija nodded again. "And you made me see the truth. That

I didn't need that book anymore. Its wise counsel lives right here." Ilija put his hand over his heart.

"Huh," said Adam. "I wanted to see you squirm, and instead you offer me gratitude?"

Ilija moved closer to Adam. Adam thought about stepping back and away from him, but instead remained where he was. Ilija carefully put his arms around Adam's shockingly smooth and white exterior. It was a lifeless shell he rode around in, but Ilija's gesture, showing him simple respect and consideration, softened what might have been his heart in another incarnation.

"You still want me to place bibles in motel rooms?" said Adam.

Ilija pulled away from Adam and nodded his head. "Now more than ever," he said. "You have wisdom, Adam. I believe it came from the most divine source there ever was or ever will be."

Adam looked around campus. Its rolling hills and imposing buildings were the only home he had truly known since he got resurrected. Now, under this tree, heavy with life, he saw something he had not seen before: the buildings were a blight on the landscape. They spoiled the wild perfection of nature, even the nature that had been artificially concocted here.

Maybe it was time to step out of the garden.

"I'll do it," said Adam.

Ilija put his hands together and brought them to his lips.

"Thank you," he whispered. Adam wasn't sure if he was thanking God or Adam, but in the end decided it didn't really matter.

Ilija bent down and began raking up the scraps of the bible with his extended fingers. "Let's clean this up," he said.

Adam dropped his torso down and placed his knees on the grass and supported himself with whirring motors as he helped Ilija collect the litter he had deposited on the grounds of his eden.

Adam held a box of bibles in his hand, balancing them like the wind might balance a rock: with ease born of a perfect fit to the assignment one has been given in life. He stood next to Ilija in a small office of the Note L Motel outside Tucson, Arizona. The sign by the road bore a logo consisting of a stylized letter "L" made to look like a musical note. Adam thought it a rather clever image for such a straightforward business. After all, there was no doubt as to what this Motel offered its customers. The manager looked at them both with an air of amusement.

"Not too many of my guests need a bible," he said. "In fact, I'd guess most of them would just as soon not be reminded that there even *are* bibles."

"Even so, Mr.—?" said Ilija.

"Name's Justin," said the manager.

"Mr. Justin," said Ilija. "Even so, it's a free service. We

place one of these volumes in each of your rooms, the daily rated ones as well as the hourly rated ones, and if any of your guests should ever feel the urge to better their spiritual existence, they will have the means at hand."

"Well, whatever," said Justin, smirking. "Most of my guests are not here to further their spiritual experience."

"I see. You're saying they are here for more physical pursuits."

Justin laughed. "You might say that."

"But Mr. Justin," said Ilija, "How do we know they would not seek spiritual solace if we—that is, you—do not offer them the opportunity?"

"Why do you think I would care, one way or the other?"

"If nothing else," said Adam, "you could advertise that the bibles were placed by a robot. People seem to like that sort of thing."

Justin waved his hand in a dismissive gesture. "Okay, okay. Just leave the box here. I'll have the maid put them in the rooms."

"We would very much like to do it ourselves," said Ilija.

"What? You and that pile of bolts?" said Justin, indicating Adam.

"We find that many managers—through no fault of their own, of course, since motel managers are busy people with many tasks to attend to in running their business—generally do not place the bibles. Even with the best of intentions."

Justin studied himself in Adam's chest. Then looked Ilija up and down. "You two are quite a pair."

"We have been partnering in this endeavor for almost a year now. One of the most rewarding years of my life. Up to now."

"You don't say," said Justin.

"Indeed," said Ilija.

"I heard about this one." He indicated Adam with a dismissive sweep of his hand. "He's a trick, isn't he? He isn't what they say he is. He's not some ghost come back from the dead?"

Adam shifted his weight from one mechanical foot to the other. "I assure you, sir," said Adam, "I am exactly what the press has said of me. I am a ghost in a machine."

"So you pass out these Bible books because God is great, and all that, but God didn't make you. Some crazy scientist made you. Am I right?"

"God works through many hands," said Ilija.

Adam nodded. "What my friend says has merit. I am not personally acquainted with God, but by all accounts, he is working all the time."

"Behind the scenes?" said Justin.

"Yes."

Justin laughed. "Now I think I've seen everything. A fucking robot evangelist." He raised his hands. "Hallelujah!" He tilted his head back and talked to the ceiling. "Praise the Lord God almighty! I am saved!" He dropped his head and looked at Adam. "You work quick," he said. "I'm already a believer." He laughed again, then stared at Adam with a wide grin on his face.

"That's good news," said Adam.

Ilija cleared his throat.

"I hear the lord's name a lot in this place," said Justin. "The walls, you know, they're pretty thin. People say things in the middle of their—" he glanced at Ilija "—activities. Sure sounds like divine intervention when they say the word."

"You can say the word in front of me," said Ilija. "I am aware of the fact that people engage in fornication."

"There's lots of that *fornication* going on in that book of yours, isn't there?"

"Some," said Ilija evenly.

"That where you learn about it?"

"The Bible has much to teach. On all variety of topics. All the important topics."

Justin focused his attention on Adam. "What about you?" he asked.

"What about me?"

"Why do you believe in God?"

"I'm not exactly sure I do," said Adam.

"But you're distributing his handbook."

"It's a job," said Adam, brightly.

"My colleague," said Ilija, "is still searching. We're both pilgrims for the truth."

Justin smirked at them. "Good luck with that," he said.

"Thank you," said Ilija.

Justin shook his head rapidly. "I don't know about you two, not completely, but you seem harmless enough. Here's a master key." He opened his desk drawer and retrieved a card with several holes punched in it and handed it to Ilija. "Stay out of rooms 6 and 14. They have guests. All the others are empty right now. It's our slow time, middle of the day." He grinned.

Ilija took the card and thanked him and he and Adam left the manager's office and trundled down the sidewalk toward the row of closed doors.

"He's right, you know," said Adam.

"About what?"

"No one coming here will be interested in a bible."

"You can't say that for sure. There may be an opportunity here to save someone's soul. We should not let the possibility slip away."

In the year that Adam and Ilija had been placing Bibles, Adam had grown to respect Ilija's perseverance. The man had unflagging energy for his task and his enthusiasm was contagious enough for Adam to stick with him.

They had started in Eastern Washington and spent the months since working their way down through Oregon and California, searching out and stopping at various tiny motels along the road and convincing the owners to put bibles in the rooms. They often met with reluctance at first, but Ilija invariably convinced them that what they were doing was a good thing. Not one ever refused.

Periodically, Ilija placed orders with a printing operation somewhere back east, which shipped boxes of Bibles to various post offices along the way. At first Ilija picked up the boxes and loaded them into their beat up old van, but he soon saw the advantage to his old tired muscles and bones of having Adam do the heavy lifting. Adam was glad to help, and always got stares at the post office. He contorted his face into a wide grin on those occasions.

The postal employees seemed to love him. They asked if he would deliver the mail on their routes. "Another time," said Adam on those occasions. Often, people waiting in line would step aside for him to be served before them. This touched Adam, and a few times he found himself saying "Thank you and God bless." in response to those gestures of courtesy.

People often responded in kind, but not always. Sometimes his statement was answered with a blank, or even a fearful stare.

"Just picking up my bibles," he would say.

For the first few months the press followed Ilija and Adam on their pilgrimage. But after the story became monotonous, they all, one by one, abandoned Adam and Ilija, until, finally, about six months into their partnership, they found themselves alone on the highway with no tv truck following behind.

Adam himself, after once being an internationally known news story, had fallen out of notice by most of the world. This did not trouble him. He was glad to have the time to himself, untroubled by prying eyes and personal questions.

He was vaguely aware that the resurrection program was in the public eye occasionally, but Adam had no interest in following the news. His life was simple, for now: accompany Ilija and put bibles in motel rooms.

Ilija stuck the key into the first door of the Note L Motel and pushed it open. Adam entered the room with his box of Bibles while Ilija continued down the sidewalk to the next door.

Adam dropped the box onto the bed and pulled out one of the bibles. The room had a shabby feel to it, with peeling wallpaper, worn carpeting, and scratched furniture. The tv looked twenty years old. There was a night stand, however.

Every hotel room Adam had ever been in, however rudimentary, had a dresser or a night stand, usually both, and this one was no exception, despite its squalid air of debauchery. He pulled the drawer open.

Before he put the bible into the drawer, he flipped the volume open to the last page and held it open in one hand. He moved the index finger of his other hand to his elbow joint where he touched a bit of oil that tended to accumulate there.

He didn't get a lot of it, just enough to dampen his finger tip. Then he pressed the dollop of oil onto the lower right corner of the inside back cover of the bible. He had taken to doing this soon after he began working with Ilija. Ilija encouraged it.

He said people would see this smudge and believe that the Bible had been touched by something divine.

"You are a divine being," said Ilija. "Remember that."

"Everyone's a divine being," said Adam.

"Yes, but you need to remember that you are too."

"I remember. Or, at least, I'm making myself believe."

"Good," said Ilija.

After he had applied the oil, he snapped the book closed, slid it into the drawer of the nightstand, and picked up his box of Bibles and stepped out of the room and closed the door behind him.

By this time Ilija had most of the other doors open. The line of rooms extended down the motel façade like a row of mouse holes.

Adam turned to continue his task, and was completely surprised to see Charlie standing in front of him.

"Don't you guys ever answer your phones?" he said.

"We gave them up months ago," said Adam.

"Well, it makes it hell to try to find out what you're doing."

"We know that," said Adam.

Charlie sighed and ran his hands through his hair. "You can't just stay out of touch like this," said Charlie. "I'm here to take you back to the lab. Finale and Deed want to talk to you."

"Really?" said Adam. He saw Ilija coming back from opening doors. He had an angry expression on his face, like he wanted Charlie gone.

"There's more," said Charlie.

"Yes?"

"Your parents want to see you, too."

Adam, at first, was not interested. "I don't care about my parents," he said to Charlie. "Or the mad scientists. I have a new life now."

"I know that," said Charlie. "You have complete autonomy. But who gave you that autonomy? Your parents and Deed and Finale, that's who. Think about it. It wouldn't take hardly any of your time. You can go back to your—" here he paused and almost sneered, though was able to keep it down to a mild suggestion of contempt rather than an all out show of scorn and disgust "—life's work right after it."

"I'd have to ask Ilija." said Adam.

"We'll set the whole thing up," said Charlie. "They really want to spend time with you. It'll be one day out of your life. You can give them one day. *One day*, Adam. Come on."

"It depends on Ilija," said Adam.

"What hold does that wrinkled old fart have on you, anyway?" said Charlie.

"He understands me and appreciates me," said Adam.

By this time Ilija, who had been hobbling over to them, finally arrived next to Adam and placed his open palm on Adam's back. "Sir," he said to Charlie. "You are interfering with our task."

Charlie rolled his eyes. "No interference," he said. "I simply brought a message to Adam."

"And what message is that?"

"He'll tell you," said Charlie, who stepped back from them both and stood by his car with his arms folded over his chest. He looked away from them and the motel and studied the Catalina Mountains in the distance, brown and green, with a kind of melancholy dustiness to them, as though they had been dried in an oven and put out to cool. Their jagged line cut across the sky, deep blue behind it.

Adam saw that Charlie was enraptured by the line of the mountains, and found himself engaged by the locus of the points where blue met brown.

"What's he talking about?" said Ilija to Adam.

"He says Finale and Deed and my parents want to see me."

Ilija's eyes lit up. "Indeed?" He stroked his beard thoughtfully. "This is a new development. Very intriguing?"

"Should I do it?"

"That's up to you, Adam."

"It is? I thought you were kind of guiding me in my life."

"I don't know where you got that idea. I'm no guide. More of a follower, really."

"No," said Adam. "You started me on this path. You said placing bibles is a meditative calling."

"I said that," said Ilija, "but I never indicated that you *had* to do it. I thought it would be good for you, but, Adam, you have to decide for yourself what you want to do with your one God-given life."

"Only it's not God-given, is it?"

"You've been asking that question for some time. Have you come closer to an answer for yourself?"

Adam felt the weight of the box of bibles in his hand. His servo motors, of course, had no problem handling the load, but something in his heart, his ghostly heart, still there like a phantom limb tugging at his soul, refused to carry the burden any longer. He put the box down on the sidewalk of the Note L Motel. He waved at Charlie, calling him over.

Charlie pushed himself off the car and came over.

"Well?" he said.

"I'll do it," said Adam.

"I'll set it up," said Charlie.

"On one condition," said Adam.

"Okay."

"Ilija comes with me."

Adam's eyes barely flickered. "Fine," he said.

Adam nodded. "Good."

"There's one other thing," said Charlie.

Adam felt Ilija shift his weight beside him. "Yes," said Adam.

"They didn't want me to tell you until you agreed to the meeting."

"What is it?" said Ilija.

"Deed is sick. His doctors are giving him no more than three months to live."

Charlie got in contact with all parties involved and arranged a meeting two days hence at a bed and breakfast east of Tucson, near the Saguaro National Forest.

"Hard to believe they're all coming to see me," said Adam to Ilija. They resumed their bible placing activities, scouting the city of Tucson for small motels and talking the managers into letting them place their oil-stained bibles in their rooms.

"I thought Charlie came here to take you away from your calling," said Ilija. "But he's not a bad fellow at all."

"No," said Adam. "He's just doing a job. He's okay. I feel bad about Deed."

"You should know that this meeting is probably not going to be an idle reunion," said Ilija.

"What do you mean?"

"He's going to want something from you. He's going to feel entitled."

"I have nothing for him."

"Maybe not. But you should be prepared."

Adam had no idea what "prepared" could possible mean. They finished their placements for the day and spent the night in the van, as they usually did, at a roadside rest area with Ilija sleeping in the back and Adam folded into the passengers seat, powered down, to allow his ghost time to rest. Adam's ghostly aspect still needed sleep, of a sort. It was not exactly the same as when he was alive but it bore some similarity. There was the same dreamy loss of perception, and the feeling that time had passed without him being aware of it but the loss of awareness was not quite complete. He felt rather like he was swimming through soupy water during these rest times. He wanted to dream, just to have something interesting and entertaining to amuse himself, but never did. He reflected that perhaps *he* was a dream himself, and this gave him not a feeling of deprivation or inadequacy, but rather a sensation of exaltation. To be a dream. Nothing seemed more wondrous than that. He felt like it brought him closer to creation and he accepted the sensation as a gift, never wanting to diminish it or allow himself to denigrate it.

Ilija snored behind him, wedged in between boxes of Bibles on either side of him. The snoring was a cacophonous sound filling the van completely. Adam could have blocked it out.

Charlie, when he had come to him with news of Deed's condition, had also given him a means of controlling his own auditory functions. But Charlie did not want to block the snores. They gave him something else to think about during his resting phases. Ilija loved him enough to accept him for what he was.

No one else seemed to want to do that. They all saw him as something else, something foreign, something to be avoided. Even the ones who made him.

This was not necessarily a terrible thing, but it was a difficult way to be in the world.

Ilija awoke near dawn. Adam prepared a breakfast of coffee and a warm bagel for him using a small microwave oven that Ilija had installed in the van to make it more like home. As Ilija ate, he thanked Adam for the humble meal.

"Bread and water, right?" said Adam.

"Indeed," said Ilija. "Although I don't know what Jesus would have thought about coffee. It rather adulterates the water, doesn't it?"

"You're saying coffee is a sin?" said Adam.

Ilija laughed. "Not at all. I was just playing with the idea of bread and water."

Adam nodded. "Do we have our itinerary for today?"

"We're not going to place Bibles today," said Ilija.

"Why not? It's not Sunday, is it?"

"No. Tuesday. You're going to meet your makers tomorrow."

Adam contorted his face into a laugh. "Not *that* maker, surely," he said.

Ilija saw the humor but did not laugh. "I think you need some time to reflect on what this meeting will mean. I think it would be best if you take a day of rest and gather your thoughts and your strength." Ilija dipped the last of his bagel into the last of the coffee in his cup and popped the soggy morsel into his mouth.

"I trust your judgement," said Adam. "As I always do, but I don't know what I need to reflect on."

"I'll take you out to the desert," said Ilija.

"The desert."

"That's where we are. You know, most of the Bible takes place in the desert."

"I know that," said Adam.

"There's wisdom here. Spiritual enlightenment. The desert is so stark and prickly. Tough. You have to pay attention here. It makes you see that there is something beyond this life. It sharpens everything. It's no wonder our spiritual foundation began in the desert."

"I'm not sure I see exactly what you're getting at."

Ilija climbed forward from the back of the van, leaving his rumpled bedsheets behind, and slid in behind the steering wheel. "You'll see," he said as he turned the key and backed the van out of its parking place.

Adam looked out the window as they passed land studded with low-lying mesquite trees, twisted as though gusts of wind had wrung them dry like dish cloths. They took an exit toward the outskirts of Tucson and travelled up a long and lonely road.

Just as the sun began to peak over the horizon Ilija pulled

the van over near a park entrance. They got out of the van and walked over to the entrance, an area with a chain link fence and a sign bearing a warning about mountain lions in the area.

Adam saw the sign and instantly felt fear strike at him. There were mountain lions here?

Ilija must have sensed his trepidation. Or seen it. "Don't worry," he said. "I'm too old and gristly to interest a carnivore, and you're, well, you're made of plastic and metal, right?"

"Right," said Adam, who on occasion still needed to be reminded of the fact, even thought at other times he wished he could forget that same fact.

They shuffled through the entrance gate and Ilija shivered. "It's cold this morning," he said.

"It won't last," said Adam. "The sun's going to be bright."

The park ahead of them displayed several trails radiating in various directions. A metal post with a lidded metal box was stuck in the ground at the confluence of the trails.

"What's this?" said Adam.

"Lift it," said Ilija.

Adam grasped the handle on the front and swung the lid up and open. It squealed in a shiver-inducing rasp. Adam found a sheaf of papers inside where people wrote down their names, where they were from, and how many were in their party.

"The park likes to know who's been on their trails," said

Ilija. "Think of it as a roster of the faithful. People come here to hike, but they don't know they're really here for a pilgrimage. They're looking for beauty, even in this harsh landscape."

Adam saw that there were many visitors from Arizona, of course, but also some from other states and other countries. A party of four from Kenya. A family of three from London. A couple, (with horses!) from Montreal. The horses were named Nellie and Oilcan. Adam picked up the pen beside the papers and with painstaking motions wrote in his and Ilija's name. In the "Location" column he wrote "Earthly plane," then closed the lid.

Ilija put his hand on Adam's lower arm joint and guided him along the path, then took up a position in front of Adam. Dust came up in clouds around their feet.

"Hope that doesn't clog up my works," said Adam.

"Don't worry about it," said Ilija.

"I do worry," said Adam. "I don't have the regenerative capacities that you have."

Ilija didn't answer.

They passed more mesquite trees and trees with bright green bark. "Those are palo verde trees," said Ilija. "They've adapted themselves to this environment by moving their energy collection from their leaves to their bark."

"Huh," said Adam.

"All living things find a way to glorify the bounty of God."

They continued walking. The trail was covered in small

rocks, a slippery scree that Adam had to navigate carefully to keep from falling over. Hikers passed them going in the opposite direction back to the trailhead. Adam noted some surprised expressions, but no one stopped to talk to him, or paused to admire their reflections in his chest. They seemed content to let Adam and Ilija continue on their way.

Ilija kept up a continuous chatter, pointing out the different cactus they passed. "Those are barrel cactus," he said, pointing to a low green blob covered in lines of thorns. "And that there is jumping cholla." Adam followed his finger to a strange plant constructed of finger-length segments loosely attached to one another. Each segment had a fearsome arsenal of very sharp and very closely clustered thorns. Ilija stepped off the trail and stood beside the plant.

"You don't want to touch the thorns," said Ilija, "because they have tiny hooks on the tip that grab onto you and won't let go."

"I see," said Adam.

"Not that that would happen to you."

Adam nodded.

"But look here," said Ilija. "He extended his index finger and touched the very tip of one of the segments and jostled it gingerly for a couple of seconds until it detached itself from the main plant and fell to the ground."

"That came off pretty easily," said Adam. "Is the whole thing put together like that?"

Ilija nodded. "It's designed that way so the segments will

stick to passing animals. Then later when the animal shakes it off it'll put down roots where it falls and start a new plant."

"You're making that up," said Adam.

Ilija shook his head vigorously. "No, Adam. I'm not. There's a lesson for all of us here."

Adam made his face laugh. "What lesson is that, old man?"

"Don't get attached to anything. Even yourself."

"So I should let chunks of me go?"

"In a manner of speaking." Ilija stepped back onto the trail and led the way from the trailhead deeper into the desert. Adam noted a hilly section that looked like it was miles in front of them. They continued walking for a time.

"Are we going up to the mountains?" said Adam.

"Not that far. Do you see the saguaro?"

How could he miss them? They were everywhere. The tallest plants visible, by a long way, they rose up from the desert floor and extended arms out from their main trunks which bent and extended up.

They looked uncannily like arms. The skin was a deep green, arranged in furrows that ran down the length of the arms and trunks. Rows of thorns adorned the length of the furrow peaks from the very top, where they clustered into a blurry mass, to the bottom, where roots were visible looping up from out of the ground like writhing snakes.

"The saguaro are like accordions," said Ilija. "They expand

at their folds when they get rain, soaking up the water, then contract when it gets drier."

Adam noted holes dug into some of the arms and asked Ilija about them.

"Those are bird holes," said Ilija.

"Do they hurt the saguaro?"

Ilija laughed. "No," he said. "The birds and the cactus get along."

"All God's creatures, right?" said Adam.

"Something like that. Now look down at the bottom of that one."

Adam followed Ilija's pointing finger again and saw a particularly ravaged saguaro with some of its flesh taken away. By what, Adam didn't know. Disease? Birds? Other creatures? Old age, maybe? How long did Saguaro's live?

"What happened to it?" said Adam.

Ilija shrugged. "Frost, maybe. Sometimes they get damaged by frost. It gets down to freezing sometimes here in the winter. But I want you to look closer. Look inside."

Adam bent forward and peered at the cactus.

"Go on," said Ilija. "Go off the trail. Get a closer look."

Adam extended his foot from the dusty path to the untrod ground that reminded him of kitty litter with its tiny rocks spread over the dry earth. "Didn't it say to stay on the trails?" said Adam.

"Don't worry about it. Who's going to know?"

Adam took several more steps toward the cactus. The tiny

rocks scrunched and squealed under his feet. He stopped, not wanting to disturb the quiet around him.

"That's the ground telling you hello," said Ilija. "It's a pleasant greeting. Acknowledge it."

Adam murmured a soft hello back to the ground.

"That's the idea," said Ilija. "Have you got a good look yet?"

Adam brushed past jumping cholla, and pushed aside some palo verde branches that hung in his way. They scraped along his exterior. "What am I looking for?" he said to Ilija.

"You'll see it when you get to it," said his mentor, who knew a lot more about desert plants than Adam would ever have thought.

He stopped a few feet from the saguaro and looked up. The thing towered at least thirty feet above him.

Its skin, which looked soft and pliable from a distance, now revealed itself to be leathery and tough. Without asking permission from Ilija or the plant, he recklessly put his finger up and touched the green valley between the rows of thorns. His finger barely indented the skin. It was tough, like him. An exterior that kept everything away.

"Now look down," said Ilija.

Adam dropped to his knees and looked at the damaged section that Ilija had pointed out from the trail.

It looked exactly like some creature had come along and taken huge bites out of the trunk. The flesh had scabbed over, not with the leathery green skin, but with some bark-like grey layers of palm-sized wafers. Adam looked beyond that to the center of the wound.

He wasn't sure he saw what he thought he saw, not at first, then realized that the interior of the cactus was not fleshy plant material, as he had assumed, but wood.

He scrambled to get closer, dragging his robot body as close as it would get, as close as he could make his eyes approach the struts embedded in the center of the cactus.

His head hit the edge of the wound. He turned on the light attached to the top of his forehead and lit up the struts. The cactus had a skeletal structure.

"Do you see it?" said Ilija.

"I see the bones of it," said Adam.

"Hah!" said Ilija. "Bones. Yes. The natives from this area think of the saguaro as people because they're built like us. They have a skeleton wrapped in flesh."

Adam pulled his head back to allow room for his arm to reach into the wound and he placed his fingertips on the wooden rods. He felt a deep affinity for this plant.

He felt it held mystery and wonder.

His ghostly essence swirled around in his robot shell, wanting to break free and find some physical connection with the standing person buried in the saguaro.

He thought of his first memory after his resurrection. How the picture of his own circuitry presented wonder and mystery. He felt that same sensation now, as he contemplated the interior of this cactus, adorning this dry landscape.

He felt pressure on his back. Ilija's hand.

"They're amazing," said Adam.

"That they are," said Ilija. "When you stand up on a ridge and look across the park, you see them, thousands of them, towering above the other plants on the ground, holding up their arms to the sky. It's very inspiring. I can't help thinking they're reaching for God."

Adam dropped his fingers from the wound, put his hands down on the ground and pushed himself up to a standing position. "Do you think they have any conception of God?" he said to Ilija. "They're plants."

"I don't underestimate any part of nature," said Ilija. "Not one. I don't underestimate a bug, or a rock, or the lowliest weed. I think there may even be divinity in a piece of scat."

He kicked at something round and dry on the ground, dung left by some desert creature. Maybe a coyote.

The thing arced up into the air and landed some distance away.

A jack rabbit, implausible with its over large ears and hind legs, bounded into their view, paused, then galloped off into the maze of cholla, saguaro, mesquite, and prickly pear.

"I even," said Ilija, "think there's divinity in you. Now my task is to convince you of that."

"What makes you think I don't think that already?" said Adam.

"You don't walk like someone who thinks he belongs in the world," said Ilija.

"That's because I'm stuck in a robot," said Adam.

"A weak excuse," said Ilija. "You could move more fluidly if you wished to do so."

"You don't know what you're talking about," said Adam.

"I had a car once," said Ilija. "A long time ago. It was a regular car. Metal and plastic and glass. An engine, a transmission, wheels, and so on. It was put together just like any other car, but it had *something* no other car had. It had attitude, and presence, and it moved like it had a life of its own."

"You're saying I'm like a car?"

"Not exactly. But in a manner of speaking, yes. Adam, you're the first one of your kind. You should be a leader."

"No one wants me to be their leader."

"I want you to go into that meeting tomorrow with your head held high and your soul in control. Can you do that?"

Adam didn't know if he could. He didn't know if he even knew what that meant.

He gestured at the wounded saguaro behind him. "Is that why you brought me here, to make me think I'm a saguaro? Or a car? Or—what?"

"I brought you here to show you the mystery of life. To show you you are part of that mystery."

He stepped closer to Adam and put his arm across his back and leaned close to him.

Adam felt only the gulf between them, made of hardware. His soul struggled to push out from the center of the robot and burst through the exterior, but it didn't happen. Not then.

Peter, the man hired by Deed and Finale to mediate the meeting, had his nose stuck so far up into the air that Adam wondered if the poor man might be close to breaking his own neck. He regarded Ilija with a cold eye. "Your presence was not requested," he said.

The three of them, Adam, Ilija, and Peter, stood in the sun in front of the house that Charlie had directed them to, a one-story adobe structure behind a black iron fence, set on a slope of the Catalina Mountains and overlooking the sprawling expanse of Tucson spread out below them like a stain on the desert. Saguaros and mesquite trees studded the yard. The front of the house displayed windows with bars and a sign indicating that the premises were protected by an alarm system. A low-hanging porch lent the forbidding façade an air of counterfeit homeyness. Peter's slightly ridiculous contemptuous air added to the general phony feel of the house and the grounds surrounding it.

Ilija and Adam were late. Not too late, but enough to let the others know they had the power to make them wait. That was on Ilija's recommendation which Adam was happy to go along with. He had no objection to showing any of these people that he could be in charge if he wanted to be.

"Ilija is here as my advocate," said Adam.

"I'll have to check this with Doctor Deed," said Peter.

"You go do that," said Ilija. "We'll wait here. Make it easier to leave if they don't let us in."

Peter lifted his chin even higher, if that was possible, and looked at Ilija with what he must have hoped was a withering look. Ilija looked back without blinking. Adam did the same, although it was easy for him.

Peter huffed out a small breath then turned from them and entered the house.

"Kind of a high strung guy," said Adam.

"He's got a job to do," said Ilija. "Like all of us. Don't worry, he'll let us in. They want you here. I come with you. A package deal."

"I'm not worried," said Adam. He stepped out from the shade of the porch until he stood in the full sunlight. It streamed down on his exterior. His sensors registered the energy as heat and he welcomed the feel of it, bathing himself in the rays like he was taking a shower in it.

"Sometimes I wish I never came back," he said to Ilija.

"Why?"

"I don't fit. This isn't life. Not really. It's some kind of simulation of life."

"Any life is better than no life. You got sent here for a reason."

"What's that reason? To put Bibles in sleazy hotels?"

Ilija raised his head so the sun shone on his face. "I will

tell you, truly, that my time with you has been the most rewarding of my life," he said.

"That's hard to believe," said Adam.

"You were sent here for a reason. You were not created by Deed or Finale. They were merely the instruments of your resurrection. Do you understand that?"

"Resurrection, resurrection. I hate that word. I'm not like Jesus, okay?"

"I never said you were."

"I'm not your savior."

"Of course not. You're an exalted being, as are all beings. All things, living or dead. All things that are not things as well."

"You are very peculiar," said Adam. "I think that's why I hang around with you."

"Are you prepared to meet your creator?"

"You mean Deed?"

"No."

Adam allowed his brain to consider other alternatives. "My parents?"

"No."

"The collider that fished me out of the ether?"

"No, Adam. You're thinking too much."

Adam attempted to stop thinking, but found it impossible. There were always thoughts floating around in his brain. If he even had a brain. What was he now? He spent many hours attempting to figure that out but never got anywhere.

His probing of the question almost always resulted in him getting dizzy or bored. Sometimes both.

The door squealed open behind them. They turned. Peter looked them both up and down, barely controlling his disdain.

"They say they will allow you—" he nodded at Ilija "—to attend the meeting."

"Told you," said Ilija.

"Follow me."

Peter turned and went through the doorway and down a few steps to an expansive front room. Adam and Ilija followed. The floor was laid out in one -square-foot stones. Adam let his feet drag, so they clanked and scraped on the stone, just to make the sound more irritating to Peter, who obliged Adam's mischief by turning his head and staring at Adam's feet with unrestrained contempt.

"I'm the reason for this meeting," said Adam to Peter.

"I am aware of that."

"No need to be so disagreeable to me."

"I assure you," said Peter, "I am nothing of the kind. I am here as a mediator."

"I wanted to ask you about that," said Ilija. "What are you here to mediate? What is this meeting about?"

Peter took two or three more steps. He stopped and faced them. "Wait here," he said.

Then he disappeared into a hallway off to the side and Adam and Ilija were again left alone.

"It's a nice house," said Ilija. "I could be comfortable here."

"I like our van better," said Adam.

"That's because comfort isn't important to you. You can be anywhere you want."

"Anything wrong with that?"

"Not a thing. Do you feel any trepidation ahead of this meeting?" said Ilija. "Do you anticipate anything approaching discomfort or emotional hardship?"

"Not since I discovered God."

"Very funny," said Ilija. "He's going to want something from you."

"Who? God?"

"Cut with the jokes. I'm talking about Deed."

"There's nothing I can give him."

"Maybe. Maybe not. In any case, I want you to let me do the talking."

"Why? Are you smarter than me? Do you know more about what I need than I do?"

"What's gotten into you?" said Ilija.

Adam repeatedly kicked at one of the stone squares on the floor until a corner of it chipped off.

"Stop that," said Ilija. "You're not a child."

"We're all children," said Adam. "That's what I've learned since my return. You, me, my professors, Deed. My parents. All children. None of us is equipped to maturely face the world. I cling to my old life as an architecture student, then hook up with you to spread the word of a so-called supreme being who is anything but. You're so afraid of the world, you hide behind stories and pretend you're helping people. Deed needs to make a walking talking toy he can point to and say 'Aren't I grand,' holding me up to the world like he's a kid showing his mommy the latest bunny rabbit he made out of clay."

Ilija grabbed him by both shoulders. His hands slipped off and scraped across Adam's shiny surface, sending up screeching sounds, like he was dragging his fingernails across a chalkboard. "Look," he said, "get a hold of yourself. You're not going to do yourself any favors by being in this state when you meet Deed. You're not a school kid getting sent to the principal's office."

"Blah blah blah," said Adam. "You don't know what it's like in here. I'm always trying to get out. Do you know that? My smoke keeps trying to squeeze onto the other side of the mirror. But it gets stuck and trapped back inside, where all it can do is poke at the leverage points and make me twitch and squirm. It's disgusting, is what it is."

Peter returned to the room. "They are ready for you," he said.

Adam stopped talking. He felt Ilija's hands, still on him, as though they were insects intent on drawing out his blood. Blood he didn't have any more. He made his body shudder until Ilija noticed and removed his hands and stuffed them in his pocket. "Remember what I said," he muttered under his breath.

Adam made no indication that he had heard him. They followed Peter into a room off the hall, where a large table filled most of the space. Several people sat in chairs arranged around the table. Adam recognized his parents, who did not look up at him. Charlie sat next to them. Beside him, two men: the one on the left was very thin and looked weak. The one on the right was large and imposing. Peter introduced them as Doctors Deed and Finale. A sixth person, a woman in a nurse's uniform, sat next to Deed. "This is Queenie," said Peter. "Dr. Deed's nurse. Dr. Deed is very ill and requires around the clock attention."

"Never mind that," said Dr. Deed. He stood up, which obviously took a lot out of him, and extended his hand. "Let me shake the hand of the first person to be brought back from the dead," he said.

Adam made no motion to move closer to Deed. "We said there would be no direct contact between the parties," said Peter.

"Screw that," said Deed. "I want to shake Adam's hand. The whole world does, why not me?"

Finale looked embarrassed. Adam couldn't tell if it was in sympathy with Deed or with Adam. He felt only contempt and resentment from Deed. Who was this slip of a man to be expecting anything from Adam? Hadn't he done enough by unceremoniously ripping him from his natural endgame?

"I think Peter is correct," said Ilija, stepping in front of Adam. Adam, briefly, wanted to bring his arm down on Ilija's head, but the impulse passed and he settled back in his enclosure, slightly amused by Ilija's earnestness. Adam noted Peter's eyebrows raised a bit, as if to suggest that perhaps Ilija wasn't quite the rube Peter had thought he was.

"I let you come to this meeting," said Deed, "but I didn't expect you to interfere."

"No interference," said Ilija. "It's just that you did not lay out the parameters of the meeting, so we need to protect ourselves."

Deed, evidently overcome by his exertions, gingerly settled back in his chair. Nurse Queenie moved to his side and checked his pulse.

"Before we go on," said Ilija, "I would like Adam to reconnect with his parents."

"It's not necessary," said Adam.

"It is," said Ilija.

"I agree with your representative," said Peter. "We'll give you a few moments."

"But they don't *want* to," said Adam.

Peter pressed his lips together and shook his head. Adam's mother looked up at him. Her eyes were red. His father had his arm around her. He wanted to think of them as his Mom and Dad, but he could not. They were Roberta and Steven. Two decent people, by all accounts, but they were nothing to him anymore. They could not be, because he was no longer a person. Not a real person. Not someone born like a real person was born.

"It's not that, son," said Steven.

"Then what?" said Adam. "It's okay, you know. I don't particularly want to know you, either. It's strange. Ever since you disowned me, it's been okay. I've gotten along fine. And you don't need to see your own son like this. It's like seeing a monster."

"Now, Adam," said Ilija. "We talked about this."

"We saw pictures," said Roberta in a voice shrill and cutting, as though she was shredding air. It rang and echoed in the room, then everything went very quiet. "Before we were supposed to come see you, they sent us pictures. Just for us to get used to—you."

"Okay," he said. "You saw pictures of me. Was I so awful? They made me look pretty lifelike, I thought. Think."

"Try to understand," said Steven. "We didn't want to abandon you, but it was just too hard on us. We remember you as a strong young man. Not—" He didn't finish.

"Not this monster," said Adam. "Is that what you were going to say."

"I don't even know if you're really in there," said Roberta.

Again, a heavy silence filled the room.

"Perhaps we should try this another day," said Peter.

"Then why did you come today?" said Adam.

Roberta and Steven both looked at Deed, now slouched in his chair. Finale studied Adam carefully, like he was examining a tire for excessive wear. "You wear my robot well," said Finale.

"Never mind that," said Adam. "Let's get to it."

"Yes," said Ilija. "Let's."

"You all know I'm dying," said Deed.

"It's been in all the papers," said Ilija evenly.

"It has not," said Peter.

"I know," said Ilija. "But it should be. All of Adam's life has been publicized, ad infinitum, until he got to the point that he needed to withdraw from the world for a time and help me in my work."

"Ah, yes," said Deed. "Distributing Bibles, right? Is that really proper work for a modern marvel of technology?"

Ilija spread his hands and made his eyes go wide. "And what better way to spend one's time?"

"I gave him that time," said Deed.

"With no strings attached."

Deed had no response, beyond clamping his jaws as tightly as his weakened state would allow, and staring glumly at Adam.

"I think," said Peter, "it might be best for all parties to state their demands."

"Demands?" said Ilija. "What demands?"

"I need that robot he's wearing," said Deed. This time the silence that descended on the room seemed more final than when Roberta spoke.

"I'm using it," said Adam.

"No you're not," said Deed. "*He's* using it." Deed pointed at Ilija. "He's using *you*."

Ilija lifted his chest so he rose to his full stature. "I have not enslaved Adam."

"Oh?" said Deed. His voice, weak to begin with, grew even quieter and developed a kind of rattle that unnerved Adam.

Charlie, completely silent until now, looked at Adam and mouthed some words. Adam thought he was saying "I'm sorry," but he couldn't be sure.

"Go ahead," said Ilija. "Ask him."

Deed turned to Adam. "Do you know what the Bible is?" he said.

"I have an idea," said Adam.

"It's a slave's manual. The whole culture it sprung from was based on slave labor. The virtues it extols are slave virtues. Obedience and acquiescence to the rich and powerful."

"No!" said Ilija. "That's a ridiculous interpretation."

"Oh, really?" said Deed. He nodded to Charlie, who rose from his chair and retreated to a closet against the far wall. He grabbed a box from the closet and heaved it onto the table. It fell with a thump. Then he got another box, just as heavy, and dropped it onto the table as well.

"Know that those are?" said Deed.

"If I had to guess," said Ilija. "I'd say they were Bibles."

"Very good," said Deed. "Charlie will bring out a few more."

Charlie did exactly that, depositing three more boxes onto the table. His face was red with the exertion. He sat back in his chair.

"It's nice to have such loyal employees," said Deed, "that they'll do anything for you."

Charlie made a point of looking away from Adam.

"Now," said Deed. "You open those boxes and you'll find Bibles. Dozens of them. In all different languages. I've made a hobby of collecting Bibles. Bet you didn't know that, did you? Started when I was a kid and my parents made me read the damn thing. I liked it, though. A great tragic story. A being with great power creates the most wondrous world and creatures. Then they all go wrong. Fall into sin. Do unspeakable acts. Wither and die. Maybe the saddest story ever written because everything God ever made eventually up and died.

"I identified with the poor sap, even when I was a kid, because I knew I was going to create things too. And I took the Bible to be a cautionary tale. I was going to create things that were much more pure and would never have the taint of corruption about them."

Adam listened carefully, transfixed.

"With me so far?" he asked not just Adam, but everyone in the room. No one answered, but he continued anyway.

"See, the Bibles, all of them, in all their translated glory, they reinforced my convictions. I've got a Bible in Spanish, in Swahili, Navajo, Klingon, Esperanto, and Basque. I've got

Bibles in thousands of languages. Did you know it's the most translated text ever?"

He was quivering with—something. Adam could not tell if it was passion or anger. Maybe both. His voice was still weak, as though there was no air behind it, but that did not keep it from filling the room. Adam listened to the words, but he was more impressed by how Deed was managing to hold the room.

"And you know what all those translations tell me?"

"No," said Adam.

"That everyone knows what the Bible means. It speaks to everyone and says the same thing to everyone. In any language."

"It's the word of God," said Ilija. "Of course to speaks to all people."

Deed laughed. A dry, croaking sound.

"Where was God when I asked him to take away this damn lung cancer eating away at me? Huh?"

"I don't know the mind of God," said Ilija.

"But you think you know his handbook."

Ilija opened his mouth as though to say something, then thought better of it.

"Why are we here?" said Adam.

Deed looked momentarily confused. He motioned to Peter, who hurried over to his side and leaned close to Deed. Ilija nudged Adam. Adam bent close to Ilija. "Don't agree to anything," said Ilija in a whisper. "He's up to something."

"You think?" whispered Adam.

"Good," said Ilija. "You are almost as sharp as I gave you credit for."

Adam didn't know how to take that comment. Ilija thought he was stupid all these months?

"Finale cleared his throat. "We don't want this to get ugly," he said.

"Neither do we," said Ilija. "So I think we'll just take our leave now."

"Wait!" Roberta.

"Yes?" said Ilija.

"We've kept him from you too long."

"Who?" said Adam.

Roberta got up and went to another door on the other side of the room. She opened it and disappeared down the hall. Peter looked at everyone in turn. Everyone looked at him blankly except for Deed, who was intent on maintaining his stern outlook but having difficulty making it appear convincing. "This is not exactly the way I had envisioned this meeting going," said Peter.

"Charlie," said Adam. "I thought you were my friend. You said that, once, didn't you?"

Charlie tilted his head slightly and raised his shoulders even more slightly. "I have to make a living," he said.

"And Deed pays you handsomely, is that it?"

"That's it," said Charlie quietly.

Roberta returned to the meeting room. She had a leash in

her hand. At the other end of the leash, a border collie, *Adam's* border collie, who he had named Titanium, walked behind her, sniffing at the chair legs and wagging his tail. Immediately, Adam's smoke loosened from his leverage points and his apparatus sagged noticeably. Everyone in the room noticed it except Titanium. Roberta released Titanium and bent down and hugged him and aimed him in the direction of Adam. Adam struggled to get his bearings back. He rallied his smoke and tried to make it flow over his interior. It was working, after a fashion, but it was a hard struggle. Ilija's hand pressed against his back and his chest, and Ilija tried to straighten him out but he wasn't helping. Not really. He was not strong enough to move Adam's bulky and heavy body. Titanium came over to Adam, pressed his nose against his foot, his clunky metal foot, then turned away and went to Finale, who, somewhat reluctantly, let his hand drop to a spot behind Titanium's ear where he scratched for a few seconds.

"What is this?" said Ilija.

If Adam still had lungs, they would have gasped for air.

"We thought Adam might want to know what he was missing from his former life."

"We kept Titanium," said Steven, "because he was the nearest thing to you that we had left."

"He doesn't know me anymore," said Adam.

"But you know him. He misses you all the time. He still thinks you'll be coming home. He watches for you."

"I'm right here," said Adam.

"No," said Finale. "You're not."

"Here's what we're proposing," said Deed. "You give up your apparatus and go back to the way you were."

"You mean dead," said Ilija. "You want him dead."

"Death is different now than how we used to understand it," said Deed. "In death Adam had an existence."

"He was ghost," said Ilija. "That's not an existence."

"The fact that we called him back proves there was," said Finale.

"You can't make him," said Ilija.

"I won't have to," said Deed. He turned to Adam. "Adam," he said.

"Yes," said Adam.

"Are you happy?"

"Don't answer that," said Ilija.

"Are you?" said Finale.

"Don't say anything more," said Adam. "Any of you. I'm here because you want my suit, is that it? You want me out of it?"

Peter cleared his throat and attempted to take control of the proceedings. "We thought it best for everyone."

"But that's what it is? You bring me back, stuff me into this thing, and now you say, forget about it. It's all over."

"I'm dying," said Deed.

"Oh," said Adam. "You're dying? There's a support group for that. It's called Everyone Who's Ever Been Alive. They meet all the time and try to convince each other it isn't true. They like to use books like these—" Adam grabbed a few of the translated Bibles and tossed them across the room so they hit the wall and slid down to the floor. Everyone in the room flinched except Deed.

"They've tried to fit me into some of the other robots," he said. "They don't work. I can't get any purchase on the leverage points. Not like you can in yours. None of the one's after you are working. Did you know that?"

"That's not true," said Ilija. "We've seen the news stories about them. You have dozens."

Deed shook his head. "All fakes. They're just robots going through pre-programmed motions. We thought we would figure out the reasons you worked and incorporate those into the subsequent models, but Adam, they never worked. Your suit works, and only yours."

"It's like God broke the mold after he made me," said Adam.

"Exactly," said Finale.

"But you don't even want the apparatus," said Deed. "Do you?"

"It could be more to my liking."

"So why not let it go? Return to your former existence."

"So you can move in."

"Yes. We own it, you know. You're just renting, in a manner of speaking. In fact, you're getting free rent."

Here Peter's face turned red, completely losing his composure. Adam guessed that Deed just said something they had decided before the meeting would not be a good idea to mention.

"What if I refuse?" said Adam.

"We could simply stop maintaining the thing."

"And then it would deteriorate to the point that it wouldn't host me anymore."

Deed spread his hands. "Something like that."

"But you wouldn't get to use it then, either."

"And neither would you. We'd both lose. Our way, one of us wins."

"You are evil people," said Ilija.

"What do you know about it?" said Finale.

"Evil," said Ilija. "I know it when I see it. Or when I smell it."

"This is not productive," said Peter. "Dr. Deed is offering you something of value."

"And what's that?" said Adam.

"The chance at normalcy."

"Defining normal as something which dies."

Peter didn't smile. "As you yourself just indicated, that is a normal state of being."

Adam pointed at Deed. "He doesn't want normalcy. He wants to live forever."

Deed leaned across the table, as much as his condition would allow, which wasn't very far. Adam did feel a pang of pity for him. Any creature that required so much effort simply to make himself known and felt by others deserved some kind of consideration. Or so he felt at that moment. He chose not to contradict Deed, or offer anything in the way of an impediment to his words or actions. Deed seemed to him no more than a dying insect writhing on the ground. This insight gave him no particular pleasure, except the contentment of finding one's self in agreement with reality. Adam missed that particular feeling. Ever since his resurrection, he had felt like he and reality had more or less parted ways and he did not like it at all. It gave him a nauseous feeling much of the time, relieved only by making his contraption go through the motions of physical labor, such as placing Bibles in motel rooms. Is that what Deed was getting at? Was he trying to say that Adam could relieve himself of the burden of trying to synch up with reality simply re relinquishing the suit?

"You've had your fun," said Deed. "Now let someone else have a crack at the thing."

"Do you even know how to do it? You got me when I was dead. You aren't dead yet."

"We have developed some methods," said Deed.

"This is ridiculous," said Ilija. "Adam is not required to give up his shell. You cannot exert any moral influence to sway him. You have no moral right."

"Wait," said Adam. His voice sounded much too loud in the room. He had nudged the volume up to make himself sound more in command than he felt. It seemed to have the desired effect: everyone in the room gave him their complete and full attention.

"Deed," he said. "You make sense. Me carrying around this thing like a snail with a high-tech shell, isn't my idea of life worth living."

"Adam!" said Ilija.

Adam moved his smoke over the leverage point for his arm and made his limb raise and spread his hand so it covered Ilija's face from his view.

"But," said Ilija.

Adam moved his hand closer to Ilija's face. Ilija backed away a few inches, as though needing to regroup. He could regroup all he wanted. He would not have what he needed to sway Adam. Not any longer.

"The only thing is," said Adam to Deed. "I don't have anything else. I have nowhere to go if I give up my shell to you. I might just as well allow it to fade into decrepitude. I would at least have *something* then, for a while. Under your scheme, I would have nothing."

"Not nothing," said Deed. "You would be able to say good bye."

Good bye? *Good bye?*

"You can't be serious," said Adam.

"I've never been more serious in my life. I've said good bye. To my colleagues. To my family."

"What family?"

"I have two ex-wives. Ulia still loves me. And I still love

her, in a way. Not as husband and wife, but as people who respect each other. My second wife, Verryl, is not so much in my heart as in my mind. We were colleagues. She is a scientist, like me. We thought that would be enough to keep us together, but it mostly made us clash. Strong egos, you see. We had a stormy two years together and then she left me for her own sanity. I said good bye to her."

He paused and looked at Adam. Was Adam supposed to feel sorry for him? Everyone died. Deed was no different.

"And I have children," said Deed, continuing. "Ulia gave birth to twins. Wade and Xandra. I have said good bye to them. Adam, you don't know how much that has meant to me. The peace it has given me. I don't have much time left. Maybe a month, maybe a little bit more. I know, once I die, that I will be separate from all of this. That was the flaw in our plan with you. We thought we could bring you back to the world, but that isn't the case, is it, Adam? You're not really a part of this world at all. You're like a visitor here. A tourist. Being a tourist is no way to live. Is it?"

Perhaps not, but then why did Deed want that existence? It must have some attraction to make him want to replace Adam. Or was it just idle scientific curiosity? Could that be enough for someone to choose the half life Adam had endured for the past few years?

"I wish I'd never come back," said Adam. "That's true. You all had no right to bring me back, then abandon me in this machine. But now I *am* back, and everything is different."

"Not really," said Deed. "Life hasn't changed. How we live our lives is still the same."

"And how we die?" said Adam.

Deed spread his hands. "It's getting late," he said. "I'm getting tired."

"We haven't resolved anything," said Ilija.

"There's nothing to resolve. We are offering Adam a return to death, which he seems to be more than a little interested in. We're glad to allow him that courtesy if he will allow us the use of his shell."

"Return to death," said Adam. "It's a nice sounding phrase, but it means nothing. I wouldn't be returning to anything. I'd have a new death to deal with. A new afterlife."

"But Adam," said Finale, "it would not be any different from your first one."

"How do you know?"

Finale looked uncomfortable. He wanted to answer, Adam could see that, but he had no good answer to offer. "We've studied the issue," he said.

"Studied it?" said Adam. "I've *lived* it. I didn't even know I was dead. Not really. I thought I was dreaming. I was in this floaty dream place that seemed to last forever. It was kind of nice, actually. Uncluttered. Clean. Everything not only in its place, but also out of sight, sound, and mind. That's what you all can look forward to, I think."

"I take exception to that," said Ilija.

"Of course you would," said Adam. "You're still invested in the book, aren't you? The paradise that's coming? I never had that. I was too young to look forward to dying. The way you do." He nodded in Deeds direction.

"I'm not welcoming it," said Deed, "but events have conspired to force me to accept it. I am embracing it."

"And why can't I embrace it, too?" said Adam.

"You've had a few years to do so," said Deed. "And you haven't been able to. I would say that's a pretty clear indication."

Adam brought his smoothly lubricated arms up and put his finely detailed hands with their precision articulated fingers up to the sides of his head. He meant the motion to be dramatic and mocking, but found that it perfectly summed up his feelings on the subject. On all the subjects they had been discussing.

"I feel like I've been shown something evil," said Adam. "This half life that you pushed on me. If only you had left me alone. All of you."

No one looked his way for a long time. Ilija's hand snaked up his back to the base of his neck. Adam wanted to feel that touch, but there was nothing to feel. No way to feel anything. He could only observe.

His smoke writhed around the cave of his existence. The smoke wanted to get out. It searched for openings in the shell, but found none. Instead it latched onto the leverage points and threw itself at them. Adam's limbs rose and fell. They twitched and writhed and jerked. He tipped over onto the floor and continued his machinations there, rolling from side to side and smashing his limbs against the chair and table legs.

"What's wrong with him?" came a voice. Several voices.

"He's working it through." Deed. Smug know-it-all.

Adam continued his tantrum, for it could be called nothing else, then, completely exhausted by his exertions, he lay stretched out on the floor. He felt like a dead creature. Road kill splattered on some anonymous highway.

"No way out," he said quietly.

Peter cleared his throat and spoke. "No way out, Adam, but they're offering you a way back."

Adam gathered his strength and smoothed out his smoke as best he could, so that it gained some semblance of order and contrived to move his internal apparatus to upright himself. It was a decidedly slow process. Deliberately so, as Adam attempted to understand the workings of each little nook and cranny held within his crypt. He rolled over so the full weight of his apparatus leaned on his chest. He moved his knees closer to his chest so that his torso began to rise. He bent his arms at such an angle that he caused his head to rise from the floor to a height comparable to his upper body. All these motions he executed with exacting and deliberate precision. Finally, he pushed himself off the floor. Heard his servo motors hoist the bulk of his frame up, pivoting on his hips. The clinks and hums and tiny squeaks sounded like the popping of fireworks. No one in the room aided him in his machinations. Adam thought maybe they were afraid of him. And why not? He was a weighty and imposing construct of heavy materials. He could easily hurt any of them. All of them. Not that he wanted to. But he had the power. He could do it. Hurt all of them at once, if he so desired.

And did he? Did he desire to hurt them?

Adam tried to ignore the question, though it nagged at him. He had all this power. He could move so much, simply by exerting his smoke. His will. Turn mirrors into blades, as it were. Forge knives from ploughshares. He didn't have to execute his will. Just having the ability was enough to give him a feeling of infinite power.

Even though he knew that power was limited. Had to be.

Adam stood up as straight as his apparatus allowed. He should be breathing hard. He should be taking in enormous breaths. That's what was proper after the struggle he had just endured.

But he didn't breathe. Couldn't breathe.

That one fact, at that moment, filled him with an overwhelming melancholy. Where had his life gone?

He turned to Roberta. "Good bye, Mom," he said. He exerted his will over his smoke, he slid over leverage points, and swung his torso a few degrees until he faced his father, who looked up at him. Adam noted pain in his face. It was sympathy for Roberta, who stared down at the table, unwilling to look up, unwilling to face the thing that her son had become. Adam did not blame her for avoiding him, and did not blame his father for supporting her. How could it be otherwise?

"Good bye, Dad," he said.

Adam turned to Dr. Deed. "Good bye, Dr. Frankenstein," he said. Deed cracked a smile, a small one. Adam liked that. He made his face smile back.

"And you too, Dr. Finale," he said. "Good bye."

"Farewell, Adam," said Finale, with a lot of conviction behind it.

"Titanium," said Adam. "Where's Titanium?"

Peter got up from his chair and went around the table to the other side where Titanium had been tied to the table leg. Peter brought the dog close to Adam. Adam stared down at his dog, the dog he remembered, but didn't have the sense memory of holding. He moved his arm down to the dog's head

—was it getting harder to move his limbs?—

and placed it as delicately as he could on the spot at the base of Titanium's skull. He wanted to scratch his dog's skin, feel his fur through his fingers, but that would not happen. Titanium tolerated the alien touch for only a second or two, then ducked away from the hand.

Adam sighed on the inside.

No one heard his sigh. No one needed to.

He tilted his head up at the ceiling. "Good bye Professor

Barometer, measure of all things, who made me read the worst book ever written."

He put his head back down and looked at Charlie. "Good bye traitor," he said.

Charlie nodded and whispered back at him. "Good bye Adam."

Adam wanted to engage Charlie further, but Charlie looked about as embarrassed as anyone Adam had ever seen. So he let that go. Didn't need to hear anything from him anyway.

Finally, he turned to Ilija. "I think what got me the most," he said. "The first time I saw you was the white beard. Who wears a long white beard like that? No one. Except you. You reminded me of God. Do you believe that? Because it's true."

"You reminded me of God, too," said Ilija. "I thought I was seeing divine creation in you."

"Sure," said Adam. "I understand that. I *was* divine creation, even if it was Deed that fished me out of the ether. But then we went on this—what would you call it? A road trip? A pilgrimage? Something. Doesn't matter, I guess. Putting Bibles in motel rooms. What a thing for me to be doing, eh? It was like a rock trying to enlighten someone. Do you think a rock can do that?"

"I do," said Ilija.

"Remember that one manager in Idaho? What was her name?"

"Yolinda."

"That's right. Crazy name, Yolinda. She didn't want our books contaminating her rooms. Remember that?"

"Of course," said Ilija.

"What she wanted us to do, instead of putting the Bibles in the rooms, she wanted us to put rocks in the rooms. Oh, that was so funny. I wanted to laugh. I wanted to have sides that could hurt, you know? Because the funny thing was, you didn't want to do it. Said it was sacrilegious."

"That I did," said Ilija.

"Yeah. The manager of a crappy hotel in Nowhere, Idaho, telling you about what was sinful and what wasn't."

"I thought of the desk drawers we placed the Bibles in as miniature altars."

"And why wouldn't you put a rock on an altar?"

"A very good question," said Ilija. "You asked me that question then and I didn't have an answer for you until later. I thought about it and decided you had a point. Rocks *did* belong on altars."

"And oil."

"And oil," said Ilija.

Finale perked up at the other end of the table. "Oil?" he said.

"I put a finger tip of oil on each Bible before placing it," said Adam. "My signature."

"Your sign that you were there," said Finale.

"Exactly," said Adam.

"A little bit of hubris there, isn't it?" said Deed.

"Maybe," said Adam.

"I like it," said Deed.

"I'm not a bit surprised," said Adam.

"You leave any oil on the rock?" said Finale.

"No. Just the Bible. I liked marring it. Made me feel better about the whole thing. Ilija convinced Yolinda to do both. He'd place a rock if she'd let him place a Bible. It was a kind of dance between them. They had something going, you know, some kind of flirtation thing, her telling him what he could and couldn't do, him trying to push for something more than she would allow. It was funny to watch."

"It wasn't funny to be a part of," said Ilija. "We had a good streak going. No one had refused us and then she came along and she was a tough one to crack."

"But we did it," said Adam.

"We did. Ultimately, everyone we approached finally agreed."

"And what does this have to do with anything?" said Deed.

"It's been my life's work," said Adam. "I want to reminisce about it."

"Adam," said Ilija. "You don't have to do any of this. You don't have to give up your shell. You don't have to go back to that darkness."

"You don't think I was in heaven?" said Adam.

"Not if you're here," said Ilija.

"It was a blankness," said Adam. "But it was comfortable,

you know. It felt *right*. This doesn't feel right. My parents are correct. They don't recognize me as their son because I'm not their son. I don't know what I am."

Ilija stared him in the face. "You're made from the Earth. Just like all of us."

"Not like all of you. Not even like that cactus you showed me. That cactus was alive. I'm just a simulation of life. Goodbye Ilija."

No answer for a long time from his partner. Adam waited. His smoke trembled inside his shell. The leverage points suddenly felt more prominent than they had up to now in his resurrection. They felt like peaks in a mountain range, arrayed for his benefit. His smoke moved, swirled. It vibrated and slammed against the inner walls of the shell. Adam began to feel dizzy. He became a whirlwind spinning inside himself. His smoke twisted and twirled and tightened and compacted, turning all his energy back on himself until the smoke that was his essence coalesced to a dense vibrating core of spirit. He was aware of his apparatus teetering and trembling because he had vacated the control and leverage points.

He now floated inside, separate from the shell, arguably more himself than he had been in months. People in the room scrambled to come to his aid. He laughed at their antics. They were people trying to assist a contraption. What could they do? Nothing. Nothing for him any longer. The robot was losing its balance. Ilija, sitting beside him, did not move away.

Adam's vision, the last thing he had left of his connection to the shell, began to darken, just as the robot teetered over past the tipping point, and, unhinged from Adam's will, began a descent that would bring it directly atop Ilija's head.

Adam, poised as he was in a sweet spot in the center of his shell, tried to undo the knot that he had become, but he knew it was too late.

Finale shouted at Ilija. Adam heard it as a faint whisper. Peter and Charlie were coming over to grab him and pull him away. They had frightened looks on their faces. They didn't want this little old man to be crushed under the weight of Adam's apparatus, but it was already too late. Anyone could see that.

He wanted to hear Ilija's goodbye, but that, apparently, was not part of the plan. The cosmic plan that Adam knew had to be there, somewhere.

Didn't it?

The robot picked up speed as it fell under the divine guidance of the laws of gravity. Adam retreated from his unraveling and tightened his being to a hard nucleus. As the shell arced downward this nucleus, this inexplicable dot of will that he had become, remained fixed while the shell slipped past him and in an instant he was released from it, free to roam. Free to be. Free to trip outside of what he had been.

He had no sense of sound or sight.

Which is not to say that he did not have *vision*. He could see, all right. He could see the great expansive wave of creation arrayed around him like a dark hall of mystery: no features, just an emptiness that he could fall into if he needed to. And he needed to. This time he was aware of what was happening to him, knew his destination. He would avoid the vicinity of particle accelerators, that was for sure. No need to be brought back to the realm he just vacated.

There was something, though, tugging at him. A strange kind of force pulling at his being. He did not recognize the source, but knew Ilija would probably have attributed the sensation to God. But Ilija thought everything originated with God and Adam knew that wasn't true. Couldn't be true. He had been here before and seen no evidence of the being Ilija believed in so strongly.

No, the energy Adam experienced had its origin in something much older and more permanent than any deity. It had the singular weight of something so ancient it had no name but many aspects.

Other beings resided here. They floated, like he did, in an expanse without features and so they reached for—something—in the void.

Adam moved his smoke towards the forces gathering on the horizon.

He was in a particularly vulnerable state now, with no leverage points to anchor himself. He was a snail without its shell. An animal with only the sky for shelter, and what shelter was that?

Other smokes, other remnants of life energy, rolled around in the void and some of them came within his vicinity.

They contacted him.

At first Adam pulled away, gathering up his smoke in a protective move born of instinct. But the time for that instinct was dissolved. His smoke was not vulnerable, so he let himself feel the other presences that were attempting to insinuate themselves on him. Gently, of course.

And then a flash of recognition hit him like a hammer. This was Charlie. Right next to him, flowing around Adam and through Adam and into Adam's being like a surrogate heart pumping blood through Adam's smoke, smoke that no longer needed blood, no longer needed anything to live, since living was an abstract notion now. Wasn't it?

Wasn't life just an afterthought here? An artifact of being in a place that required physical means of locomotion?

Adam's mind reeled from the implications. How could he even be thinking these things? He had no physical presence any longer.

But this was Charlie. Unmistakably him. He was a munching, eating, annoying presence. *There* in a way he remembered from his previous life, now so separate from him that it felt like ancient history. How could something that happened thousands of years ago still be relevant to Adam now?

He exerted his will. He asked Charlie why he was here.

I miss you, Adam.

Oh what a thing to say to smoke. What a thing to think about smoke.

Best to let me go, Charlie.

He moved away from that presence and was confronted with another: weak and faltering. *Thank you for letting me have your shell.*

Deed's fake gratitude.

You'll like it for a while, but in the end you'll hate it.

That felt good to say.

He pushed away from Deed. Such an unpleasant presence. In both realms. He wanted to peel away the feel of him. If he had hands he would slide them over his arms and shake the dripping sliminess of Deed from him. But he didn't need to do that. All he did was offer his will to the void and Deed receded from him, a thoroughly minor creator, scrambling for the shell Adam had discarded, trying to hold onto his life for no good reason that Adam could see.

And then two presences floated to him. Two familiar smokes, bound by a bond he could not quite see, but which he knew was there. Adam paused, not willing to let these two go. They held a familiarity for him. Two voices, separate but working in harmony.

Adam. Is it you?

Yes Mom. Yes Dad. It's me.

They floated close, nudged at him. They wanted his attention, nothing more. A small reminder they could keep.

He obliged, sliding his smoke into their vicinities. He sensed surprise. Then joy.

How can this be? His mother's voice. *Is it really you, Adam? Can it be you? We were so frightened of what we did, but it is you, isn't it?*

Yes, Mom, it's me.

Adam waited, imagining that in the physical realm his mother was crying, tears salting her cheeks, gasps convulsing her body.

Goodbye Adam. Goodbye goodbye goodbye. We're so sorry we brought you back. Will you have peace now? Can you?

I don't know. I'll try.

His father, also there, offered only stoic silence. Adam accepted it as his version of farewell.

Goodbye Dad.

Bon voyage, Son.

A proper farewell, then. A meeting of souls for an instant. A true meeting unmitigated by the physics of the fleshy realm pushing air over vocal chords. What did that have to do with a meeting of the spirit?

And then he pulled away from those presences, those smokes, still tied to physical bodies, to their own versions of shells. It wouldn't last, this need they had for anchoring themselves to physical things. It would pass. As his need had passed.

And now, one more broken being to attend to.

His smoke twitched. He felt like he was descending and rising at the same time and recognized the sensation as his being lost in the void, but knowing exactly where he was lost.

Adam?

Yes, Ilija.

It's wonderful, what you had. You shouldn't have let it go.

I had nothing. Just a mechanical contraption.

It fell on me. As you left.

I know. Did it kill you?

Yes, but but but. It also didn't. I'm in it now.

Adam wanted to laugh. He had a tiny regret he no longer could. But that regret passed in an instant.

What about Deed? He wanted it.

Tough luck for him. Finders keepers.

I don't remember that as one of the commandments.

We sometimes use our own commandments.

He's going to fight you.

Let him. All he can offer is death. How is that, by the way?

You'll find out soon enough.

I suppose you're right. I'm liking these leverage points. This is going to be fun. I'm rising up on my feet now. I'm going to look menacing to Deed and Finale. Deed is going to be so mad. So mad.

I expect you're right. Thanks for making my life trivial.

You're welcome. Thanks for validating my ridiculous ideas about you and what you should be doing.

Adam wanted laughter again. But still it eluded him. No matter. He disconnected from Ilija's presence and slipped, one last time, over the leverage points of the robotic costume that Deed and Finale had constructed for him. He moved away from the assembled souls, who had all come together to convince him of—what? His temporary existence? No need to convince him of that. He already knew it.

And now, one last tug. A strange smoke. Small and wiry. Too small to hold a human, yet big enough to engulf one. It crawled up onto his own smoke, tendrils of it intertwining with his, and an inquisitive dampness, like the air after a rain, but warm. Maybe a touch repulsive, except the kind of repulsion that disappears with strong attachments.

Adam floated close to Titanium. Exalted creature, unencumbered by the knowledge of what comes after. Or what won't.

Goodbye Titanium.

An overwhelming force of affection enveloped Adam. The kind of unconditional love that dogs can't help offering.

Now why did I dismiss you so easily?

Adam reveled in the joy of this creature, in the unrelenting *there*ness of its capacity for experience.

Oh Titanium, I misnamed you.

Adam felt the pull of the broad expansive ether, taking

him from his dog. He did not fight it. The pull was greater than anything. Any force, any love, any *thing*.

Yes, Titanium. You are not of the physical realm at all. You should not be named for a metal. I hereby correct my error and name you for a spark, a spirit, a pure energy.

Goodbye and farewell, Zap.

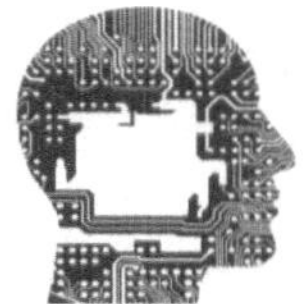

You just have read **The Ghost and the Machine** by Emen. Copyright © 2019 by Emen.

ISBN: 978-1-949644-56-2

This book by Emen. No fair for you to be copying this book, so don't do it, okay.

Picture of robotic head profile: © Gordon Johnson | Pixabay

Emen no dedicate books so don't ask him for to dedicate book to you, okay.

Other books by Emen:
Assa's Eggs • The Institute • Thieves • 20 Weird Love Stories

About the author:
Emen born in faraway country, never mind the name. Is old news now. Emen not chicken of spring. No. He is older man. Born long time ago. Now have white beard. Like man made of wisdom. Or like Santa Clause. Choice is made by you and your imagination. Emen have big respect for users of imagination. Also is having big respect for peoples who read books. Is not necessary for good life to read books. But can be fun. Imagination is good. Imagination bring Emen here from old country.